IN THE CITY
BY THE SEA

KAMILA SHAMSIE

BLOOMSBURY PUBLISHING
LONDON • OXFORD • NEW YORK • NEW DELHI • SYDNEY

BLOOMSBURY PUBLISHING
Bloomsbury Publishing Plc
50 Bedford Square, London, WC1B 3DP, UK

BLOOMSBURY, BLOOMSBURY PUBLISHING and the Diana logo are trade-
marks of Bloomsbury Publishing Plc

First published in Great Britain 1998
This edition published 2018

A catalogue record for this book is available from the British Library.

ISBN: PB: 978-1-5266-0783-6; eBook: 978-1-4088-2598-3

2 4 6 8 10 9 7 5 3 1

Printed and bound in Great Britain by CPI Group (UK) Ltd, Croydon CR0 4YY

To find out more about our authors and books visit www.bloomsbury.com and sign
up for our newsletters

For my parents
Muneeza and Saleem
and my sister,
Saman

Prologue

Newspapers kill.

At the thought, Hasan's lips stretched into the first-thing-in-the-morning smile which broke his mouth out of its sleep-imposed mould. Before the smile had achieved its potential smugness, Hasan's right hand was already moving. Fingers spread to cover maximum area, the hand reached down to the carpet, skimmed over tea-burn, yo-yo string and dried glue splotch, and bundled yesterday's comic page, sports section, TV listings and local politics page into a mass of fly swat. Hasan raised his weapon and waited, motionless. *Thwack!* His posterior jerked in remonstration at the ferocity of the assault.

'The rear forces have been decimated,' Hasan announced. 'But they gave their lives willingly in order to destroy the enemy.' He inspected the newspaper bundle. 'The enemy has been squashed.'

Hasan turned over on his back and something fluttered on to the sheet, beside his thigh. He touched his forefinger to the tip of his tongue and used the damp digit to lift the object off the sheet and hold it up to the shaft of sunlight that breached the curtains. Translucent, multi-veined gauze of onion sliver. Hasan sighed, and the wing blew off his finger, twirling in unencumbered flight. Hasan had a fleeting notion of raiding all the neighbourhood kitchens for onions, which he would unravel and stitch together into giant wings, but then he recalled that he couldn't stitch. Plus, there was the smell factor to take into account.

'Oh, well,' he said, extricating himself from his cocoon of sheets and peering under the bed. 'Only one week to mid-term holidays, Yorker,' he announced to the stuffed toy with smiling cricket-ball head and batsman's garb which lay sprawled atop a pair of sneakers. Yorker's smile had come unstitched at one end, giving him a downturned pout that made Hasan instantly guilty as he recalled his failure to stand up to his cousin Najam's taunts the previous evening.

'Okay, sorry,' he said, placing Yorker on his bed. 'Most stuffed toys are for babies, but you're different. And I'll say as much to the next fourteen-year-old idiot who tries to insult you.' Hasan pushed up the corner of Yorker's mouth and fixed it in place with a thumb tack. 'Look, a dimple!'

Hasan swung himself out of bed. 'One week more,' he repeated, enunciating the words to the point of distortion. He closed his eyes to savour each syllable, feel the inrush of air and swelling of cheeks to 'one', taste the explosion of 'week-kkk' in the back of his mouth, smell the drawn-out exhalation of 'more'. Smell the drawn-out exhalation? Hasan wrinkled his nose. No, that was morning breath. He ran his tongue over his gums, regretting his decision not to brush his teeth the night before so that he could awaken with the taste of *rubri* still in his mouth.

2

I must be getting old, he thought. I'm worrying about hygiene.

The notion was so distressing that Hasan resolved not to brush his teeth for the rest of the weekend, but then he happened to look across at the cluster of posters stuck with studied haphazardness on the wall above his desk. Amidst all the poses of all the figures in open-collared white shirts and white trousers, one stood out. Hasan's favourite cricketer, that magician with his willow wand, square-cutter of the full-toss, driver of the outswinger, sweeper of the googly: Raza 'Razzledazzle' Mirza. In the poster Razzledazzle was bereft of both his bat and his famous reversible two-fingered gesture of victory or abuse. Instead he held up a toothpaste box emblazoned 'Plaqattaq' and beamed ear to ear, revealing whiter-than-nature-intended teeth. 'Get yourself a full set of cricketing whites' the slogan advised.

Hasan trudged to the bathroom.

Minutes later, scrubbed and dressed in *kurta* and jeans, Hasan switched off the air-conditioner, and hopskipjumped out of his bedroom. In the hallway, Ami's *Reclining Nude* had been replaced by *Still Life with Flowers*, one of the many paintings gifted to Ami by exhibitors at her gallery and subsequently relegated to the storeroom.

Hasan put his need for breakfast on hold, and poked his head into his parents' room. 'Who's coming over?' he whispered.

Aba reached over to his bedside table with his left hand, felt around for his stopwatch, scribbled something into the morning paper's crossword grid, paused the stopwatch, and looked up at Hasan. 'Client,' he mouthed.

'Conservative type?' Hasan said, gesturing towards the still life in the hall.

3

'I am to be seen, through a cracked open door, kneeling on my prayer-mat when he arrives,' Ami said, her eyes flickering open.

'Nonsense,' said Aba. 'You're to serve tea, and ask how else you might be of assistance, keeping in mind your female limitations. Ow! Ouch! Sorry! Sorry! Sorry!'

Ami kept a tuft of Aba's hair twisted around her index finger, but stopped pulling it. 'Is he grovelling?'

Hasan shook his head. 'Just begging. Give him another second or so.' He darted out of the room before Aba's cry of 'Ingrate!' could thump him between the shoulder blades.

In the kitchen, someone who was either the new cook or a thief was piling the dining room silver – fruit bowl, tea-set with elongated teapot, cake-slicer, horse figurine, candelabra – on to a table, his back towards the door. Hasan skulked in the doorway. Or tried to. He wasn't quite sure what 'skulk' meant, but the configuration of letters suggested 'to sneak like a skull'. Hasan sucked in his cheeks and crouched low, beneath a grown man's eye level. The man whipped out a rag and silver polish from a cabinet.

'I'm Hasan,' Hasan said in Urdu, advancing into the kitchen. 'And you are?'

'Yes,' came the reply. 'I am.'

'God is great,' Hasan said, with the confidence of someone who knows he has the last word. He procured a glass of milk, an empty bowl and a whole pomegranate from fridge, crockery cabinet and, after some searching, spice cupboard, and pushed through the screen door.

The sun was ferocious, a taste of the summer months ahead. Along the boundary wall purple, orange and pink bougainvillaea flowers drooped their heads and attempted to curl beneath their own leaves, and the hibiscus flowers in the back

4

garden let hang their pollen-tipped tongues. Hasan's jeans clung to his legs as he made his way to the back garden and up the spiral staircase to the roof.

The *mali* next door saw Hasan sit cross-legged and sweating beneath the overhang of the rooftop water-tank, and turned his garden hose away from Uncle Latif's prize *chikoo* trees. He pointed the hose upward and pressed his thumb against the hose's mouth, constricting and rechannelling the flow of water. Two streams of sun-sparkling transparency spurted out from the sides of the hose and arced towards Hasan. The cement roof hissed on impact; snakes of dust stirred, but the steady jet beat them down. Hasan ducked his head in thanks, raised the pomegranate above his head and smashed it against the cement.

A crack, surrounded by a purple bruise, ran down the leathery covering. Hasan squeezed his thumbs into the crack and prised the pomegranate apart. There – hundreds of teardrops encasing teardrops, crimson flesh offering no resistance and much enticement to teeth which would bite down and hit a seed that only teased with its hardness before revealing its brittleness. Hasan did not have the patience to scrape each segment from the bitter strip which held it in place. He raised one half of the pomegranate to his mouth, clamped down his teeth, felt the first explosion of juice into his mouth, and saw the boy.

The boy stood on a rooftop the next street over – within ball-throwing range if you had a good arm, and Hasan did. The boy looked about Hasan's age, slightly taller perhaps, though that impression could have been created by the thickness of his sneakers' soles. He was too intent on attempting to fly his yellow kite to notice Hasan, but the mere fact of the boy's presence at an elevation Hasan considered his own in the

5

early morning hours was enough to make Hasan put the pomegranate down and wipe his mouth.

Little gusts of wind blew past the boy, making the kite hiccup through failed take-offs.

The water on the roof evaporated; the sun inched a little closer to Hasan; pomegranate stains turned rusty on jeans; the glass of milk warmed in Hasan's grip. Still the boy tried to bring his kite to life. And just when his shoulders seemed to slump a breeze blew up from the sea.

'Yes!' Hasan exclaimed, jumping up with upstretched arms.

The kite shivered and rose. The boy ran backwards on his roof, unreeling string, yelling 'Up, Razzledazzle, up' as the paper rhombus dipped and recovered, dipped and recovered. Suddenly everything depended on the kite. Dynasties would fall, wars would break out, next Friday would never arrive if the kite did not rise to string-tautening heights. Hasan knew that and, he was sure, so did the boy. While the boy continued to move backwards in his most enviable sneakers, Hasan puffed out his cheeks and blew in the kite's direction. The two boys, as one, willed that kite up, not for one moment turning their eyes away – not to blink away the sun, not to look at the birds wheel past, not to see who was crying out below.

Not even to watch for the roof to end.

Chapter *One*

Despite the strangeness and uncertainty that pervaded his *Mamoo*'s house that mid-term holiday, what Hasan was to remember most vividly about the visit was the smell of pine-cones. The moment Aba turned the Honda Accord on to the street where his brother-in-law lived, the smell hit Hasan and quite overpowered the mingled scent of sea-air, garbage, eucalyptus and dust that no one in the City by the Sea ever noticed until it disappeared.

Hasan had never even seen a pine-cone before, but he recognized the smell by its resemblance to the air-freshener his neighbour and old family friend, Uncle Latif, had sprayed under Hasan's nose.

'Here, smell this,' Uncle Latif had said, pressing down, and down again, on the green spray-can when he learned that Hasan was going to stay with Salman Mamoo. 'Number one air-freshener, pine-scented, manufactured by Latifbhai Private Limited, and ready to take the market by storm. When you hurry and scurry down the road to your *mamoo*'s house and smell the pines you will marvel at how successfully I have captured Nature in a spray-can. I mean, all respect to God and everything, but when news of Salman Haq's pine-cone phenomenon first entered these ears I thought, Latif, what is the point of having this glorious smell up in the mountains when the majority of this country's noses are down in the city? *Hanh?*'

In truth, the air-freshener resembled the real smell of pines only in so far as sweet, oval-shaped or circular, rich brown in colour, dripping with syrup, soft but not mushy, delicious hot or cold, could resemble the actual eating of a *gulab jamun*. And, yes, Hasan would have been able to identify the pine smell even without the air-freshener. For he, too, had heard the stories of Salman Mamoo's supporters and how they had a complex, secret network that transported pine-cones down from the hills around his real home, his heart's home, and catapulted them from rooftops into his garden in the City by the Sea.

Hasan was grateful for the smell. It made him feel as though Ami, Aba and he were somewhere different, somewhere not home, and dulled the incongruity of packing bags and locking house in order to go and stay with an uncle who lived only a five-minute drive away from home. Five minutes. But this time it had taken three months to make the drive over. Three months, almost to the day, since the radio newscaster confirmed what everyone in the City already knew, and Uncle Latif clicked his tongue and said to Hasan: 'Oh, this is the news to give us the blues. I think your lunch at Salman's has been cancelled. Or rather, for I am an optimist, particularly in the presence of children, let us say it has been postponed.'

Hasan had never before known the need for presidential approval in order to reschedule a lunch with one's uncle.

He stuck his head out of the window and watched white, beige, cream cement boundary walls and white, black, grey steel gates whiz past, their bleakness relieved by roadside grass patches, flower pots, laburnum trees, palm trees and the omnipresent bougainvillaea. Of the single-storied houses only the flat roofs could be seen, rising above the wall. Even so, the hours he had spent looking down from Salman Mamoo's roof allowed Hasan to dissolve walls and nod hello to the goldfish in the rockery pool at no. 7, smile at the girl endlessly hitting a squash ball off the back wall at no. 10/1, shake his head in admiration at the BMW, Nissan Patrol and (for the servants' use) Honda Civic at no. 17–19.

But after the road curved to the left past no. 23 the walls could really have dissolved, the goldfish could have smoked cigarettes and serenaded sparrows, the girl could have swallowed the squash ball and the cars could have danced the tango, and Hasan would barely have noticed. Well, certainly the girl could have swallowed the squash ball and Hasan would barely have noticed. At any rate, having borne the three-month separation from his uncle with a restraint which surprised even him, it now required all his will power to keep still in the back seat of the car, for his legs were insisting that they could run down the road to Salman Mamoo's house, run faster than any five-year-old-car which had to slow for speed-bumps.

'Aba!' Hasan reached over to the driver's seat to shake his father's shoulder, as the house came – or rather, didn't come – into view. 'What's happened to Salman Mamoo's wall?'

'It's profitable to be a building contractor in favour with the government these days, Hasan. The government puts someone under house-arrest, and you double the height of his wall to increase that prison sensation. And all at the prisoner's expense. Ah, our glorious law-enforcers!'

'Shehryar!' Ami warned.

There they were. Olive shirts, grey trousers, upturned moustaches. Hasan had imagined all that. But he had imagined, too, that there would be more of them. A whole squad at least, standing erect and suspicious, rifles at the ready, their eyes hollowed like the President's and their mouths as disinclined as his to smile. Instead, there were only three. Two standing to either side of the gate – the sags of their shoulders suggesting that their postures would not last very long – their rifles leaning on the wall beside them; the other seated on a steel fold-up chair with his left arm thrown over the back, the index finger of his right hand propping up his rifle. A song from a popular film was blaring from a radio that Hasan couldn't see. He wished that Aba had not refused for all these months to drive past Salman Mamoo's house. The reality proved so much less threatening than his imagining.

But as soon as Hasan thought that, Aba swung the car round to face the gate.

Hasan had memorized Salman Mamoo's gate long, long ago. When Salman Mamoo was absent from the City for long stretches during the summer, Hasan would recall the latticed black metal grilles that formed the gate, and draw them on a piece of paper from Ami's sketch pad. Six horizontal strips, eight vertical strips, forming thirty-five rectangles. Every rectangle but one had a name which Hasan culled from *The Book of Myths*. So, if you looked through Thor you could see the drainpipe near the garage, which spurted great gushes of water during the monsoons; through Apollo, the mango tree which Nana had once leaned against while singing *ghazals*, in the only memory Hasan had of him; through Kali, the patch of driveway where Hasan had fallen while roller-skating and left so much blood that Aba had to keep the garden hose

10

trained on the spot for a full ten seconds before all traces were washed away; and finally, when Hasan had imagined the thirty-four named rectangles he would allow himself to think of the thirty-fifth which framed the doorway where Salman Mamoo always stood in Hasan's memory.

But now a sheet of steel had been welded on to the gate, and each rectangle led Hasan's gaze to impenetrable blackness.

Aba rolled down the car window and passed a letter to the seated army guard. 'For you,' he said. 'From the President.' He saluted.

The guard held the letter close to his face, and began to pick his teeth with a corner of the paper.

'Please,' Ami said. 'He's my brother. Let us in.'

The guard peered in at Ami, and started with surprise, hitting his head on the window-frame. Hasan smiled to himself. Ami looked so much like Salman Mamoo with her slight features, high cheekbones, and coal eyes that it was not uncommon for guards who were meant to keep Salman Mamoo inside or out of a place to wonder momentarily if Ami were Salman Mamoo in some elaborate disguise.

Another guard walked over, took the letter from the first and read it through. 'Yes, fine,' he said. 'We were told to expect you. Excuse him – he doesn't know how to behave around ladies.' He saluted, prodded the first guard to do the same, and barked out an order for the gates to be opened.

'Sorry, Saira,' Aba said, his mouth half a smile, half a grimace. 'Didn't mean to antagonize him.'

'Why can't you just break out into a sweat or start trembling like normal people do when they're nervous?' Ami said.

'Because you always said you didn't want to marry a normal man.'

Ami slapped Aba lightly on the forearm. 'Drive in, or they'll close the gates.'

Salman Mamoo was, as ever, watching them drive in, his body a diagonal in the wood door-frame. But in the scant seconds it took to leap from the car door and cut across driveway and garden into his uncle's arms, Hasan noticed that he could see the frame of the dove painting inside the house that Salman Mamoo's body usually obscured completely when he was positioned so.

'*Arre, pehlvan*, you've grown again,' Salman Mamoo laughed. 'Sorry I missed your birthday. You're into double digits now, right?'

'Salman Mamoo!' Hasan objected. 'That was last year. I'm eleven now.'

'Oho, Sal-Man, what's with the hair?' Aba leaned over Hasan to clasp Salman Mamoo around the shoulders.

'This is what happens when I'm kept away from the mountains in the winter. My supporters throw pine-cones into my garden and God sprinkles snow on to my hair. Hello, girl.'

The last words were a whisper and he repeated them, softer, as his arms stole around Ami's waist and his head rested on her shoulder so that it seemed, for a moment, as though Ami's head was growing backwards from Salman Mamoo's body. Aba caught Hasan by the shoulder and propelled him indoors. The first thing Hasan noted was that he was finally taller than the potted plant near the doorway and, next, that the white marble floor still bore the stain of a rose petal crushed beneath a stiletto heel, reminder of the celebratory night when Salman Mamoo's party won the vote of no-confidence. Aba prodded Hasan and together they walked through the wooden double doors into the lounge, hub of the family section, where the rose-water smell of Gul Mumani embraced Hasan a moment

12

before her arms did.

'Gul, Gul, Gul, when I see you my heart is garden, garden,' Aba sang out.

'Shehryar, Shehryar, Shehryar, you're making less sense than ever. But looking gorgeous. Have to say it. Look-ing gorgeous! You know, the first time I saw you I remember saying, "That boy has so many waves in his hair he could rival a sea", and now it looks as though you're competing with an ocean. But where is . . .? Sairoo!'

'You would think it had been more than a week since they last met,' Salman Mamoo commented, walking in behind Ami. 'Gul, don't suffocate my sister. You know I'll be blamed for the murder and speedily executed.'

Gul Mumani glared at him. 'Listen to him. You would think this was a joke.'

Aba clapped a hand on Salman Mamoo's shoulder as the two men sank into adjacent sofas. 'What, is't a time to jest and dally now, Salamander?'

'Etymology?' Salman Mamoo said.

'Salamander. From the Greek, *salamandre*. First meaning: a mythical animal having the power to endure fire without harm.'

'Oh, I like that! Gul, Saira, Hasan, call me Salamander.'

'Second meaning: a portable stove.'

'Gul, Saira, Hasan, call me Salamander, first meaning.'

'Ignore them, Gul,' Ami said. She reached over and took the sleeve of Gul Mumani's *kameez* between thumb and forefinger. 'Where did you get this lovely material?'

Aba and Hasan grinned at each other. However lovely the material, it was the same lemon-yellow as one-fifth of the clothes in Gul Mumani's wardrobe. When Aba and Gul Mumani were at school together, Aba would taunt Gul

Mumani with the nickname 'Pastel Cannonball' and though her size and wardrobe had changed since then, her proportions and colour choices had not.

In the fervour of describing details of how she found a cloth shop when searching for a store that sold egg whisks, and how she bargained with the cloth seller, and goodness! how the tailor nearly wrecked the outfit with the addition of sequined hems, Gul Mumani gesticulated so vigorously the clothes pin on her head sprung off and her hair cascaded down her back. Salman Mamoo and Aba both bit off their smiles, but Hasan could tell that Ami was barely aware of what was going on. Salman Mamoo extended an arm and pulled Ami off the sofa. 'Come outside,' he said. 'There's something you have to see in about a minute. You too, Hasan.'

Outside, the clouds were a dragon breathing out a red sun. 'No, not that,' Salman Mamoo said, when Hasan pointed at the sky. 'Wait.' Inside, the clock chimed one, two, three, four, five, six.

'Now!'

The sky rained pine-cones.

Chapter Two

'There's actually some poor man whose sole purpose in life is to remove the pine-cones from my lawn every evening,' Salman Mamoo said. 'Our Beloved Leader's idea. I hear it's supposed to show that the government will sweep away any acts of treason, but as far as I'm concerned it just prevents my house from being buried under a mountain of pine-cones. Oh, but just smell that!'

'What happens to the pine-cones?' Ami asked.

'They're burned in the empty plot next door. That brings back memories of home, too. Hasan, will you bring a pine-cone with you when you come in?'

Hasan waited for Ami and Salman Mamoo to walk back indoors, then lay down on the pine-cone carpet, his head pillowed on his arms. The pines pricked Hasan's body. He ran his thumb up and down the ridges of one, over and over, until there was a little red dent in his thumb.

Facing away from the house as he was, Hasan should have been able to see the sun entering its final stages of descent but

the raised walls had diminished the visible sky. Hasan wondered if the moon would haul itself high enough at night to be
visible to him. Of course, at school Mrs D. Khan tried to convince Hasan with drawings and charts that his theories about
the moon were entirely wrong, but Mrs D. Khan had not been
in the desert last summer to see the moon slung so low in the
sky that Hasan would have been able to reach up and touch
the frost of its rim if he had just had the energy to climb up the
farthest sand-dune. During that desert night, huddled around
a bonfire with the sand cool beneath his feet, Hasan realized
that the moon only ascended as high as was necessary to put
itself in skywatchers' lines of vision. Tonight, would the
promise of Hasan's and Salman Mamoo's gazes be sufficient
to propel the moon up a few extra inches?

Overhead, a kite fluttered into view. Hasan rolled over and
buried his face in the pine-cones.

Footsteps shuffled behind him. A man with a basket in one
hand, a bundle of firm twigs tied together to form a broom in
the other, squatted on his haunches in the garden. There was
something vaguely crab-like about the way he scuttled forward, one foot at a time. The broom swept a wide arc in
front of him, and pushed the pine-cones into a pile in the
center of the garden. Hasan turned to go in, but was stopped
by a low whistle from the man. Hasan turned back. The man
did not look at him, but one foot kicked a pine-cone in
Hasan's direction. Hasan pounced on it, ducked his head in
acknowledgement, and ran indoors.

Gul Mumani was still talking, her voice rising and falling in
that familiar melody that changed its tempo with her mood,
but only disappeared altogether when she tried to sing. 'And,
so then he came up to me, no! he sidled up to me, that's the
word, and said, why don't you join us in the other room,

16

we're having a very interesting political discussion. So I said, na, *baba*, na, I hate politics. He raised his eyebrows at me, so high I thought they would fly off his scalp, and said, does your husband know you feel this way? And I replied, my dear man, Salman hates politics even more than I do. Saira, when we were eighteen neither of us could ever imagine me saying this, but it gets so tiring, you know, meeting new people, wondering if they are spies or what, always watching your mouth so that you don't trip over your tongue.'

The phone rang, and Hasan darted to answer it. He had to cup a hand over one ear and press the receiver against the other ear to hear the voice at the other end through the distortion of wire-taps.

'*Arre* Hasan, is that you? Uncle Farooq here. Can I have a word with Our Saviour?'

'Uncle Farooq,' Hasan said, holding out the receiver towards Salman Mamoo. Ami jumped up from her seat and grabbed Salman Mamoo's arm. 'His brother's marrying into the President's family,' she whispered.

Salman Mamoo shook off Ami's grasp. 'For God's sake, Saira. It's Farooq.' He took the receiver from Hasan and yelled into it, '*Yaar*, where have you been, Ooqs, you globetrotter? . . . Thanks, *yaar*, but it's not so bad. I've got the family with me these days, so we're having a blast . . . No really . . . Seriously, I'm fine . . . Oh come on, Farooq, that's not my style. Nothing to be gained by wishing others ill.' He looked at Ami and shook his head slowly, side to side.

'No, no, nothing of the sort,' he continued. 'Actually, I'm finally able to indulge my fantasy of growing my armpit hair . . . Seriously, I oil and braid it every night. You have no idea how much time goes in its upkeep. And the consistency! Go on, Farooq, peel off that T-shirt and have a good look –

but only if your deodorant is effective.' Salman Mamoo grinned at Hasan, and placed a hand over Hasan's mouth to stifle his giggles. 'What can I tell you? Gul and I got into a terrible fight the other day because I used her favorite *peranda* to braid my armpit hair. Look, do me a favour – when you finish this conversation and repeat its details to your brother's future in-law ask him if he'll tell my guards to stop harassing Zahoor about the quantities of hair-oil he buys for us from the market each week.' He disconnected the phone, and sat down. 'Here, Hasan, lob it over,' he said.

Hasan threw the pine-cone upward. It hit the ceiling, bounced down in the center of the room, and somehow Salman Mamoo was lying on the floor, his hand just under the pine-cone. 'Should have been a cricketer after all,' he said, picking himself off the ground. He squeezed the pine-cone until the veins stood out on his wrist. 'This is pine-cone number one hundred. I haven't decided quite what to do with all of them. Something vaguely artistic, I think. Then, Saira, you can sell it in your gallery as political art. How is the gallery doing?'

Ami slid one long finger along the rim of her teacup. 'I've closed it down for a while. Concentrating on my own painting. The gallery was taking up too much . . . stop looking at me like that, Saloo.'

'Then stop lying to me.'

'All right. The landlord said there was some problem with the rent agreement, and I would have to close the gallery while he sorted it out, or face eviction.'

'I see.' Salman Mamoo's voice was grim, as Hasan had only heard it once before – the day he defined 'military coup' over a phone line which started crackling half-way through the conversation. 'And what exactly was the nature of this rent problem? Your relationship to a certain *persona non grata*?'

'You can't blame the landlord, Saloo,' Ami said in her older sister voice.

'I'm not. I just. . . . for one minute, if I could just . . .'

'Salman!' Gul Mumani warned.

'Oh, Gul, *jaan*, I'm not going to say anything incriminating.'

'Why not?' Hasan said. 'We won't tell anyone.'

'I know that, kiddo. But the house is bugged. Although I think I'm not supposed to know that.'

'Bugged?' Hasan said. 'Who's the bugger?'

Aba and Gul Mumani threw their heads back and roared with laughter. Ami nearly choked on her tea. Salman Mamoo lifted Hasan up, and swung him around. 'Who's the bugger?' he repeated, tears of laughter streaming down his cheek. 'Oh, that makes another three months of house-arrest bearable. Who's the bugger, indeed.'

That night, in the stillness of the bedroom, Hasan felt as though he was surrounded. People in uniform watching him, listening to every breath, wondering why he was not asleep. From the lounge he could hear Salman Mamoo's and Aba's voices raised in argument. Hasan picked up an empty glass from the table beside him, crept to the door and interposed the glass between his ear and the door.

'Here's an aside worth considering,' Aba said, his voice maddeningly calm. 'Nostalgia comes from the Greek *nostos* meaning "homecoming" – don't interrupt, Solomon, I know you know that. But here's the interesting part – it's also probably akin to the Sanskrit *nasate* which means "he approaches". So, is nostalgia about return or about standing still and watching someone else return?'

19

Salman Mamoo laughed shortly. 'I suppose you would say the latter. You like to choose the observer option, don't you, Sherry?'

Hasan could imagine Aba smiling and raising his eyebrows in appreciation.

'*Touché*, my friend. And you would like to return home and find everything unchanged, except the things you didn't like when you left. Oh, Saloo, despite all your acclaimed books about pendular time, you cheat when it comes to your own history. You think you can choose which points on the pendulum's arc to relive.'

Hasan rolled his eyes. Grown-up talk!

Aba went on, 'Yes, you'll be your uncle all over again. Same charisma, same ability to innovate, restructure and make alliances. Same everything, except you're not allergic to prawns so you'll survive the state banquet and live long enough to implement all your grand plans.'

'What, you'd be happier if I choked on a prawn ball?' Salman Mamoo laughed.

'Be new,' Aba said.

There was a sound of movement. Salman Mamoo leaning forward? Aba reaching over to clasp Salman Mamoo's shoulder? Salman Mamoo said, 'I've been checking up etymologies too, Shehryar. There's a third word connected to nostalgia. The Old English word *genasas*.'

'*Genasan*,' Aba corrected him. 'Yes. Meaning "to escape"'.

'Very tempting when you're under arrest, wouldn't you say? Too much reality can kill a man.'

Hasan returned to bed. He drifted in and out of a strange imagining where he was both himself lying on the bed, saying 'This is the verge of a dream. You would be dreaming if you were not awake' and also himself sitting in a room, saying, 'I tried to sleep, I tried. But when I tried to count sheep they turned into kites.'

It was hot in the bedroom under the covers, but Hasan knew he would start shivering if he threw off his duvet. The City's two seasons of Almost-Winter and Absolute-Summer had been coexisting these last few days to create the third season of How-Should-We-Dress? Hasan ran through the list of possible options: T-shirt, shorts, sheet and duvet (present situation – 6/10); sweatshirt, shorts, socks, sheet (forgoing the soon-to-disappear pleasure of sleeping with a duvet – 5/10); shorts, duvet (sleeping shirtless was the kind of thing cousin Najam did to show off the solitary hair growing on his chest – 1/10); T-shirt, duvet . . . this is so boring.

Hasan rose, cracked open a window. Salman Mamoo was standing in the garden, ghostly in his white *kurta-shalwar*, humming softly. Hasan wriggled into his sneakers, and slid out through the window.

'Is it horrible?' he said.

Salman Mamoo did not turn around. 'Not now, not right now. Right now, if I really wanted to escape I would climb a moonbeam out of here. Climb right up to the stars. You know, before I wanted to be a cricketer, I wanted to be an astronomer.'

Hasan followed Salman Mamoo's gaze to the moon. 'So how old were you when you decided you wanted to be a politician?'

'I'll tell you when it happens.'

Salman Mamoo picked up a shawl from the chair beside him and draped it round Hasan. They were silent for a while, staring up at the sky. Magic, Hasan thought. When he was younger he used to spend break-time hanging from the goal post at school, convinced that if he grew tall enough he would be able to reach up and touch the sky. Now he was old enough to know the futility of such aspirations, but the sky still enthralled him. During the day it was bland enough, and when the sun blazed through its insipid blueness Hasan usually wanted nothing more than to run indoors and towards creaking fans and humming air-conditioners. But at night! Oh, at night, it was something else entirely. It arced above the earth, majestic, enigmatic, revealing nothing, suggesting everything.

'There are moments, Hasan, when I like to think that the stars are bullet-holes. For every bullet shot by an oppressor there springs to life a star, with so great a radiance that it can never be put out, it can never be imprisoned. But if that really were true, the last three months in this city would have erased every trace of blackness from the sky.' Salman Mamoo tousled Hasan's hair. 'Come on, it's getting cold out here.'

'I'll crawl back in through the window in a second. Good night, Mamoojaan.'

Salman Mamoo smiled, and kissed Hasan on the forehead before turning to walk away. A moonbeam slanted in his path on the way back to the house. He walked around it.

Chapter Three

'Ku-kura-koo. Ku-kura-koo.'

Hasan swung open the kitchen door and saw Salman Mamoo poking his head out of the window and emitting strange crowing sounds from his throat.

Over the last three months visitors who arrived unannounced at tea-time to provide comfort to Ami over Salman Mamoo's predicament invariably and repeatedly insisted that prolonged confinement caused people to go 'stir crazy'. Consequently, since the mid-term visit had received the presidential stamp of approval Hasan had been steeling himself for, and was quite prepared to face, the sight of Salman Mamoo endlessly mixing cake batter. This manifestation of madness through barnyard imitations, however, made his left ear lobe wriggle. And that hadn't happened since Uncle Latif had made use of two footballs to dress in drag for a costume party.

'Bloody bird!' Salman Mamoo declared, slamming the window shut. 'Tea, Huss?'

'Uh . . . please.' Hasan sat down on a stool at the kitchen counter. 'What were you doing?'

Salman Mamoo shook his head and held a saucepan under the hot water tap. 'Even the roosters are unpunctual in this city. The one next door used to crow about forty-five minutes after sunrise, and that was bad enough, but since my walls have been raised the bird doesn't see the sun until midday and bloody hell I'm a rural boy. I can't take roosters crowing four hours after breakfast. So I try to goad it into ku-karuing with noises of my own.'

'But for all you know you could be saying in rooster-speech, "Be silent or be dinner",' Hasan said.

'True,' Salman Mamoo said. 'Very true.'

Little bubbles of water were beginning to form at the bottom of the pan. Hasan left his seat to stand by the stove while Salman Mamoo scooped up a spoonful of tea-leaves and flicked his wrist just so to deposit the leaves in the water in a perfect circle. On impact, the tea-leaves leaked a rich brown colour into the water. Another spoonful followed suit and Salman Mamoo lowered the flame. For a few minutes there would be calm.

'So,' Salman Mamoo said, cuffing Hasan's ear, 'what momentous things have been happening in your life while the President has arranged for me to catch up on my reading?'

'I've stopped eating pomegranates.'

Salman Mamoo merely nodded. 'Uh-huh. Saira told me you've been reading Greek myths. The Persephone story had the same impact on me when I first read it.'

Persephone? Hasan started to shake his head but Salman Mamoo had already turned away, distracted by the tea-leaves sinking beneath the rollicking surface of the water. Salman Mamoo whisked the pan off the flame, spooned in sugar, added half a cup of milk and placed the pan on a slightly higher flame. He bit his lip and flexed his fingers in preparation for the split-second moment of optimum boiling. Hasan rested his head on Salman Mamoo's back for an instant brief enough to create the impression that his head was merely brushing against Salman Mamoo's shirt. The tea frothed and rose in a mass of tiny bubbles, and just as it appeared to reach overflow Salman Mamoo had the pan in the air. A twist of the right wrist and tea was streaming into a mug; a twist of the left wrist and the tea poured back into the saucepan. Right twist, left twist, right twist, left twist, until the tea's sheet of steam unravelled into long threads. Hasan held his face close to the mug and felt his pores open.

' 'Morning, 'morning,' Ami greeted, yawning her way into the kitchen. 'Sally, put the kettle on. Tea is needed with a vengeance.'

'I can make my special tea for you,' Salman Mamoo offered.

'Spare me,' said Ami. 'Anyone who boils milk in tea . . . here we go again.'

Salman Mamoo's watch alarm was frantically beeping the hour. Salman Mamoo lunged past Ami to switch on the portable radio. Hasan rolled his eyes at Ami while foreign clocks chimed the hour; he had already heard that clanging three times last night. The chimes gave way to a clipped voice which conveyed an air of perfectly coiffed hair.

Hasan twisted open the biscuit jar and contented himself with dunking biscuits in his tea while humming a commercial jingle that had been banned from the airwaves. 'T. Tea, Man's fantasy/ Where oh where would woman be, if she didn't have her own T. Tea.'

Mid-bar, Hasan recalled Ami's objections to the jingle and looked up guiltily to see if she had heard him. But at that

25

instant the atmosphere in the kitchen took on the texture of bread that had soaked in milk too long. Salman Mamoo slumped on his stool with his hands spread across his face like dovetails in shadow pictures. Ami's hand commanded Hasan into silence. Two words changed the newscaster's babble into coherence.

'. . . Salman Haq's supporters clashed with police in riots around the city. The violence was precipitated by rumours that government-funded universities have been instructed to deny admission to applicants who are active supporters of Haq's Anti-Corruption Enterprise. Official reports put the death toll at seventeen, but unofficial estimates suggest that the body count could be more than twice that number.'

A biscuit fell from Hasan's fingers and disappeared into the tea. Riots around the City! Hasan heard again the school riot alarms, smelled wet mud, felt dead leaves press against his skin as he hid in a flower bed. Stay or run? His eyes darted around. The boys on the cricket pitch were running into the Senior School building through the door farthest away from Hasan. There was another door, closer to him, but as he was about to rise from the flower-bed someone slammed the door shut from inside. Hasan heard the bolts fall. The last of the cricketers ran in and the farthest door also slammed shut, as did the lab doors and the music-room doors. A staccato chanting arose from the street, followed by crashing sounds, as though dozens of hands were beating against the side of a bus. Hasan held one hand over his heart to muffle its sound. This was no drill.

Hasan's eyes swept to the gaping front gate, where the chowkidar was on his knees, tugging at the vertical bolt which anchored the gate in place. Too late. The mob rushed in.

For one terrible moment all Hasan saw was a mass of

26

bodies, running, yelling, brandishing weapons and then . . . they're just students, he realized. Their uniforms were not of some terrorist organization, but of the government-run school up the road, and their weapons were twigs, stones from the roadsides and pebbles used in hopscotch games. Hasan raised his head a little.

'This is not a time for studying. This is a time for unity,' a boy Hasan's age shouted.

And another voice: 'Close your school. Tell your students to join our rally.'

Police sirens wailed. There was a moment of absolute stillness and Hasan found himself thinking, 'My shirt must be filthy.' Then the boys turned, ran, but by now the *chowkidar* had tugged the vertical bolt out of its socket, and locked the gate. The sirens drew closer. Someone near Hasan yelled in a teacher's voice, 'Unlock it!' but the gate was already swarming with bodies – climbing and leaping, pushing and yelling.

'Quick! The wall!'

The cry came from amidst the swarm, and some two dozen boys broke away from the gate to scale the boundary walls. Hasan remembered the shards of glass embedded atop the wall at the same moment as a dozen hands pressed down on them. When Hasan opened his eyes the boys were gone, and a redness that was not betel-nut juice trailed down the walls.

Hasan stood up unsteadily. He could hear again the staccato refrain. It was fainter this time, but Hasan understood it now: 'Sal-man. Sal-man.'

A hand, ink-stained and hairy, dragged him to class, but he didn't care because he knew people were celebrating on the streets, knew the President must have invited Salman Mamoo to form the new government. Then Mrs D. Khan asked, 'Hasan, is that your neighbour outside?' and Zehra walked into class, said, 'The Widow's sent Khan to take us home,' and Mrs D. Khan let him go without protest. But Hasan still believed the news was good, though Zehra shook her head and Khan was silent as he started up the engine.

The car turned on to the main street, and Hasan blinked at the unfamiliarity of the scene. Gone: the bustle, the almost-accidents, the games of chicken between drivers and pedestrians. Gone also: the newspaper hawkers screaming out headlines that included Salman Mamoo's name, the beggars dragging deformed limbs towards car windows, the vendors selling smuggled goods on pavements, the fruitseller carving guavas into roses to show off the pink flesh. Shutters were shut at: the T-shirt stores where cool teenagers thumbed through hundreds of shirts that were identical except for the foreign designer name emblazoned across each one; the fur-shops where foreigners gaped over clothing too warm for the City's clime; the cloth-shops where merchants unravelled bolts upon bolts of cotton and linen to dazzle all eyes, especially the Widow's. In the absence of shutters, doors were locked at Aba's tailor's shop with its framed letters of recommendation from politicians long out of style.

Khan drove through the strangeness without saying a word. When Zehra and Hasan tried to elicit some information – *what Khan* yaar *why tell us please come on where's Ami where's the* Widow *why are you here what's happening is Salman Mamoo we're not babies* – Khan only said, 'I was told to bring you home. That is all I know. The rumours outnumber the flies today. Windows down, no air-conditioner.' This last piece of information was the hardest to understand, but Khan was clearly not in a mood to explain. When Hasan and Zehra tried to talk to each other Khan told them to be quiet.

The car had hurtled through three red lights before Hasan

saw that Khan was leaning sideways in the driver's seat, his head inclined towards the open window as though listening for something. Within seconds Hasan heard the ringing sound of protestors – not young boys this time – warping Salman Mamoo's name into a battle-cry. The cry was distant, but Khan slowed down slightly, looked around as though to judge its origin, and swerved on to a side street. Three more times the cry repeated itself, each time arising from a different source, and each time Khan slowed, and twice changed course. The fifth interruption was the sound of bullets, and that time Khan kept on going, pushing the needle on the speedometer farther and farther to the right.

When Khan pulled up to Zehra's house Uncle Latif and the Widow were standing outside the gate, clearly waiting for Zehra and Hasan. Uncle Latif's hair was all out of place and he kept pushing the sleeves of his *kurta* above his elbows.

'If you roll them up, they won't keep slipping down,' the Widow was saying to Uncle Latif as Hasan stepped out of the car. Uncle Latif thrust his sleeves up again and moved forward towards Hasan. Another car came tearing down the street and Ami stepped out, very calm. She took Hasan's hands in hers. 'Salman's under house arrest,' she said.

Now, three months later, Hasan smiled at the memory of his panic. Ami raised an eyebrow at him and he smoothed out his mouth. He wondered if Ami shared his relief at having Salman Mamoo so much to themselves again. No rallies to attend or speeches to write. No ribbons to cut or bribes to refuse.

Salman Mamoo passed his hands in front of his face as though signing off a prayer, and tilted his head back. He seemed about to speak, but Ami clamped a hand over his mouth and shook her head. Salman Mamoo nodded and

29

stood up. He fumbled around the back of the spice cupboard and pulled out a packet of cigarettes.

'Saloo!' Ami exclaimed. She picked up a wooden spoon from the kitchen counter and used it to flick the packet out of Salman Mamoo's hand. Within seconds Ami and Salman Mamoo were duelling with wooden spoons over possession of the cigarette packet.

'Who gets them for you?' Ami asked, thrusting forward with her spoon. 'Zahoor?'

Salman Mamoo parried the blow. 'After his wife ran off with the guy from the tobacco company! Uh-uh! Ouch!' This last regarding a wooden rap on his knuckles. 'I buy mine off the guards outside.'

'Multi-layered irony!' Ami said. 'And of course Gul doesn't know. Honestly, Saloo.'

He shrugged. 'It keeps my hands occupied.'

The spoon-swords locked, bowl to bowl. Ami, left handed, and Salman Mamoo, more conventional in his grip, stood like mirror images who had wandered apart long, long ago and now, reunited, found expressions, hair length and final chisel-marks on features altered. The whistle of the kettle startled them out of reflection.

Ami bit her lip and turned away from Salman Mamoo. 'Those things will be the death of you,' she said.

Salman Mamoo muttered a response which Hasan could not make out.

'What was that?' Ami said.

Salman Mamoo just shook his head. It was much, much later, almost five weeks later, that Hasan would realize what Salman Mamoo had said:

'Optimist.'

30

Chapter Four

It was during that mid-term week within those high, high boundary walls which, mountain-like, cut off the outside world, that Hasan rediscovered the morning dew ritual, which he used to perform when he was five.

He awoke every morning and knew, by opening his window and gulping in the air, that it was 6.30 a.m. Outside, the grass glistened with dew that had sprinkled from the wings of dusk-fairies as the sound of human eyelids opening sent them flying backwards through time-zones. Barefoot, his body trembling with the possibility of cold, Hasan ran lightly across the grass, and knelt down.

Within seconds he heard the call to prayer: '*Ashad-o-ana-illaha-il-Allah-o-akbar . . .*', the words falling from heaven like a rope that Hasan had only to grab to be pulled up into the sky. Hasan bent his torso forward so that his whole world was the sound of the *azaan* in his ears and a single blade of grass before his eyes, dew poised on its end. He bent further down, licked the dew off the grass and, with the taste of fairyland in his mouth, he whispered . . . but here the routine changed. For, while Hasan had once whispered his wishes, 'A day at the beach', 'A new cricket bat', he now only whispered 'Azeem'.

This was the only time he could think about Azeem without that strange sensation running from the pit of his stomach to the back of his throat. The only time he could safely recall last Friday when he was unable to climb down from the roof until Zehra, unquestioning, took him down by the hand as though they were four and six again and she was once more leading him past clawing, night-draped, witch-inhabited bushes into the sanctuary of lamplight and food smells.

Later that day Ami and Aba had returned from lunch at Farah Khala's and told Hasan . . . a terrible accident . . . your cousin's cousin, Azeem . . . remember Azeem from Ali Bhai's wedding three years ago . . . well, his family just moved back here . . . bought a house just near us, and today, while Azeem was flying a kite on his roof . . .

There was a photograph from that wedding, in which Hasan and Azeem crouched in one corner, oblivious to cameras, on their faces the instant friendship of two boys exchanging views on how to fly.

Hasan retraced the green stain of his footprints back across the grass, his tread a little heavier with each passing day, for he knew this perfect morning moment would end soon, as soon as he went home to his bed in direct earshot of the new mosque which crackled the *azaan* over the hiss of a loudspeaker and did not allow the Arabic to descend, petal-like, from heaven. Besides, he couldn't breakfast on dew at home with Uncle Latif liable to lean over his balcony at any moment and yell across jocular warnings against malnutrition. And if it wasn't Uncle Latif it would be Zehra, the Oldest Man, the Widow, one of the Bodyguard.

Really, Ami was the only person Hasan could bear to be watched by on those mornings. The final morning at Salman Mamoo's house she was seated on a cane chair, sketch-book in hand, when Hasan walked back across the grass to the verandah. He squeezed down beside Ami and wrapped the trailing end of her sari around his shoulders.

'I'll miss this smell,' Hasan said, inhaling the pine smell which clung to every blade of grass, every leaf, even every fruit on the kumquat tree.

'I won't,' Ami said. 'It's the smell of my miserable adolescence.' She began to enumerate on her fingers. 'It's the smell of resenting my parents for moving us up North; it's the smell of wanting to wallop Salman for his insistence on rhapsodizing over the different shades of green his eyes registered in a single Northern morning; it's the smell of rebelling just so that I could escape the category of Justagirl, though in the process I had to become Whatkindofgirl!' Ami stopped and gave a short laugh. 'Salman went on about shades of colour and I smoked in secret. Oh, perversity of fate!'

'You don't like this smell, huh?' Hasan said.

Ami kissed his hair. 'Not a lot.' Salman Mamoo crowed out of the kitchen window, and Gul Mumani wandered out on to the lawn. 'Go get some tea. I'll join you later.'

When Hasan entered the kitchen Salman Mamoo handed him a steaming cup as though this were any other day, but when Hasan dipped his tongue in the tea he tasted salt.

'Sorry if it's a little watery,' Salman Mamoo said, staring at the tine of a fork as though it held all the secrets of the universe. Hasan turned his back on Salman Mamoo, poured the tea into a plastic container and left the kitchen.

In his bedroom, tea container clasped to his chest, he squeezed his body into the window frame. He averted his eyes from the gaping suitcase on his bed, hoping that if he was still, perfectly still, Time would join him in petrification. But though his body maintained a rigidity of muscle that would impress any drill-sergeant his mind rushed on faster-faster and Time had to leap through hours in moments just to keep up with it.

'You're not the one under house-arrest.' It was Ami's voice. She and Gul Mumani sat down on the verandah chairs, holding a bowl of raisins between them, unaware of Hasan curled just feet away. 'You have the freedom to come and go, so come to our place more, don't go to visit dreary relatives.'

'Saira, what do you think, that I enjoy, what, prefer seeing Saba and Sabiha and whatnot to seeing you and Shehryar and Hasan?'

'No, I don't. That's why I don't understand it.'

'Well, it's not that I see them more often than before. It's just that I see you less. It's not a complex thing. Simple as a simile, really. How do you think Salman would feel if every evening I left him here, locked away from the world, while I went to see you and Shehryar?'

'If you were in his place . . .'

'He's not as strong. We both know that. Strong in other ways, yes. Strong like knights and martyrs, but not like the knights' and martyrs' parents.'

Hasan wrinkled his nose at the sudden image of Sir Lancelot having to be in bed by eight. No late-night jousting. No jousting at all, in fact.

'Well, what about your schools?' Ami's voice turned hard. 'Are they supposed to go around administering themselves while you sit blithely in the City playing the good wife?'

'Saira, Oscars await you! I'm fine. Fully occupied, I swear. Though let's be frankfurter – you must have dropped your

34

brain in a flowerpot somewhere or you'd realize the schools would be shut licketyspliteky if I stayed involved with them. *Chalo*, let's see what the boys are up to.'

The two women linked arms. Then, in that moment between moving out of Hasan's eyeshot and out of his earshot, Ami whispered, 'Gul, I'm scared.'

And Gul Mumani: 'Saira, I'm terrified.'

Hasan stared at the whorls in the wood of the frame, trying to memorize them so he could take with him the frame, take with him a doorway into a world of fairy-dew, take with him a space through which he could crawl into a moonlit conversation with Salman Mamoo.

The door opened and Aba walked in, bouncing a pine-cone from palm to palm.

'Pine,' he said. 'From *pinean*: to suffer. Old English.' He shook his head. 'Be careful of the symbols you adopt, Huss. They may haunt you.'

'What?'

'Nothing.' He tossed the pine-cone into Hasan's suitcase. 'Pack. Shoes at the bottom.'

Hasan raised his eyebrows at Aba. Shoes? He stared down at the sneakers on his feet. 'But what will I wear on the ride home?' he said.

'Forget I spoke,' Aba said. He disappeared into the bathroom and came out with Hasan's toothbrush and tube of Plaqattaq. Hasan packed the bottom of the suitcase with *A Star Gazer's Handbook*, *Great Cricketing Moments*, *Lord of the Rings*, *Mathematics – Book 3*, three pine-cones and – with a nonchalance that defied Aba to comment – the container of tea. Aba's gaze rested a moment on the mathematics book. Before he could remark on its uncut pages, Hasan whisked out the book and put it on his bedside. 'I think I'll finish up my homework before we leave,' he muttered, as though speaking to himself. From the closet he pulled out an armload of clothes, deposited them into the suitcase, flattened the pile with his hands and closed the lid. He laid his cricket bat and Yorker on top of the suitcase and threw his arms wide in triumph.

Aba picked up Yorker and examined him in much the way that Salman Mamoo had been examining the fork. 'Huss, I know we joke around a lot. But if there's ever something you want to talk about. Something serious . . .'

'Aba, I wouldn't do it in a house that's bugged.'

'True enough. Come on, let's find your mother. We should be leaving soon.'

But as the moment of departure came closer, everyone recoiled from it and kept recoiling so that the distance between Ami-Aba-Hasan and departure stayed constant through the day. But finally there was no more lunch and no more desire for tea or coffee or cake, and Ami and Gul Mumani won even rematches of the rematches at Trumps, both with and without cheating, and Hasan learnt to hook a bouncer for six runs, and Aba managed to catch a pine-cone in his mouth when Salman Mamoo threw it at him, and Gul Mumani remembered the song that had been playing in the background when Salman Mamoo proposed, and she sang it with gusto, and even the sun retreated behind clouds then, and so it was time.

As they walked towards the garage, Salman Mamoo said to Hasan, 'Well, I'm sure you're ready to get out of this state of seclusion.'

'No! I had so much fun this week. And I got to spend more time with you than I have in ages. None of those weird political types around.' He paused, and then admitted, 'But I do miss Zehra's puppy.'

36

'Latif's daughter, Zehra?'

'Yes. She named the puppy Ogle, after the President.'

'Ogle?'

'As in O–G–L. Our Glorious Leader.'

'Oh, *pehlvan*, I'll miss you. But why name a puppy after the President?'

'Because they're somehow connected. They have the same birthday, they both have a scar above their left eyebrow, and last week when the President was ill, so was the puppy.'

Salman Mamoo smiled. 'It seems almost natural that peculiarities like that should occur in a house where the Widow lives.'

Salman Mamoo was still smiling as Aba started the engine and everyone waved goodbye. Just as the gates were about to close behind the car, Hasan looked back to wave once again. But Salman Mamoo was not looking at him now. He was staring, instead, at the wheels of the car. And Hasan knew that the look on Salman Mamoo's face was that of a man who watches a car drive through his gate and knows he may forever have to stand in the driveway and wave to it, goodbye.

Chapter Five

Outside, the world was dust. Dust swirled the streets, filled Hasan's nostrils, weighed down the air, made every intake of breath a conscious action. The City had changed in a week. It used to be home, but now it was just a place that existed outside Salman Mamoo's house.

As Aba rounded the corner from Salman Mamoo's house Hasan saw wild shrubs squatting in empty plots of land, their brambled arms reaching out in all directions to snag, rip, rend. Black polythene bags danced around the shrubs; one leapt up, caught the end of a branch, and fluttered, flag-like. Around the shrubs, orange peel mingled with empty milk cartons, eggshells, and bones picked so clean they held no interest for the pi-dogs. A boy and a girl, about Hasan's age, wandered through the garbage, sacks slung across their backs, in search of bits of paper they could sell. The girl yelled triumphantly, held up a book – the kind Hasan used for writing homework assignments in.

Hasan rolled down the car window and flung his mathematics book towards the children. The car screeched to a halt.

'What did you just throw out?' Aba asked

'My maths book.'

'Go and pick it up right now!'

Hasan slid out of the car, closing the door behind him with a motion just short of a slam. The girl reached the book just before he did, and picked it up. She was a little taller than Hasan, and it was hard for him to know what she would look like after a bath, though the green flecks in her eyes indicated that she was a Northerner. One hand fisted on her hip, the other holding the book, she stared at Hasan in a manner quite at odds with his expectations of a dirty, barefoot girl who scrounged through garbage. With a flick of her wrist, she released the book into Hasan's hands. He opened the book to the center page, and grabbed hold of a bunch of pages, ready to pull them out and give them to her. She stopped him with a click of her tongue, and walked back into the empty plot.

'Exactly what did you think you were doing?' Aba asked, as Hasan stepped back in the car.

'You wouldn't understand. Only Salman Mamoo would.'

'Hasan!' Ami warned.

'Can we just go home.' Suddenly Hasan wanted very much to burst into tears.

'Watch your tone of voice,' Aba said.

Good, Hasan thought, I've hurt him. As Aba took his hand off the wheel to shift gears, Hasan saw the crescent scar on his palm, its whiteness startling even against Aba's fair skin, and then he was angry only at himself.

It was about two years ago that Hasan had first heard the real story of the scar. He had never really considered it before, because nine years of seeing a thing disposes you to never noticing it. But one evening he had heard Ami refer to it as 'the war wound', followed by some mention of a bomb attack. Hasan was supposed to be in bed at the time, not sitting in the garden outside the drawing room counting the stars, so he couldn't run in and ask whatwhywhen.

But the next day, during art class, when Mrs R. Khan asked the class to paint a picture of heroism Hasan drew a white crescent. Mrs R. Khan (Auntie Rukhsana outside school) beamed at the picture, and called Ami from the staff room to gush her praise. 'So young,' she said, 'but clearly so devout. None of this clichéd hero nonsense of knights and firemen and people killing themselves in order to save a dog.' When Ami failed to see why a painting of a crescent should be so impressive, Mrs R. Khan said, 'Obvious religious symbol. The crescent of Islam.'

Later that day, poolside at the Club, Ami related the conversation. Aba raised a questioning eyebrow at Hasan across a plate of soggy french fries, and Hasan leaned forward to trace Aba's scar with his index finger. 'Your war wound,' he said. 'The one you got saving us from the bomb attack.' Ami put down her glass of fresh lime with soda, and decided perhaps she was in the mood for a swim after all.

'Saira!' Aba said, 'Don't you think you should explain . . . given that you're the one who caused the misunderstanding.'

Ami looked at Aba the way she looked only at Aba and said, 'I don't really think it is a misunderstanding, Shehryar, and don't you dare drink my fresh lime while I'm gone.'

Aba looked around for diversion, but the only people in attendance were children swimming frantically around the pool yelling 'Marco' and 'Polo', teenagers in dark glasses surreptitiously lighting up cigarettes, women gossiping around canopied tables while slanting their bodies into the shade so

40

that no sun darkened their skins, workmen cleaning the yellow brick façade of the Club's residential building, and white-liveried bearers clustered around the stone bar explaining to an irate member of the Old Guard that their hearing aids were low on battery power.

'Well,' Aba said, raising Ami's glass to his lips, 'Here's the story . . .

'As you know, you were born just in time to witness the Bigger War. Now, there'll come a time when the history books will try and convince you as to the real reasons for the outbreak of war. Just remember, the war had nothing to do with politics, economics or patriotism, and everything to do with the fact that the leaders of both sides were named after fruits, and had spent their whole lives trying to escape from that ignominy. Ignominy – deep personal humiliation, derived from the words *ignorare* and *nomin*. So, yes, they wanted to escape the ignominy of their names. Neither did, but nearly half a million people died in the war that was supposed to imbue the names Chikoo and Angur with terror.

'Whatever the reasons, the City was subjected to a constant barrage of aerial bombing in the weeks just preceding the peace treaty. The jets flew so close to the ground that it was possible to see the razor-cuts on the pilots' cheeks. Poor Begum Malik used to rush outside the house every time she heard the air-raid siren, in the hope of catching sight of her son who was an air-force pilot on the other side. There are those who say there was a look of joyful recognition on her face as she stared up at that jet, just before it dropped a bomb on her, but it's hard to know if that's the truth or just a good story . . .' Something distracted Aba away from words, and Hasan followed Aba's gaze to see Ami launch herself off the high diving board and spear her body into the water. She did not emerge immediately, but skimmed the blue-tiled floor until she reached the shallow end. 'Eel!' Aba called across to her.

'Aba . . .' Hasan said.

'Hang on, I'm getting there. Well, we were living in a rented house at the time. The green one, with the window-panes that kept rattling. In those days everyone slept in the most bomb-safe places in the house, so your mother and I slept under the stairs, and you were in a cot in the corner of the drawing room that was furthest away from the windows. And one night it happened. An explosion, followed by glass shattering. I was too stunned to move for a second but your mother scrambled out from under the covers and ran to you.

'It was dark, of course. Bombs aren't kind on electricity wires, but in the moonlight she could see you lying in your cot, not a sound, not a whimper. Your blanket was covered with glass, but your face didn't have so much as one shard of glass on it. She picked you up and walked back to me. I was look-ing for the box of matches that had been knocked off the table by the force of the explosion, and when I couldn't find it I went to the dining room where I had left my lighter. I was still smoking then, had considered quitting, but war really does wonders for cigarette sales. So, anyway, I got the lighter, came back to the hallway and lit the candle.

'We couldn't believe it. There we'd been, wandering around in our bare feet, and the floor was just a sheet of glass. So much glass . . . it was as though we were living in a green-house and the glass walls had caved in. But here's the thing, Huss. Not one scratch on our feet. Not one.

'It was about three in the morning, so we decided the only sensible thing to do was to go to sleep. We went up to the bed-room, because the likelihood of another bomb falling on our street was unlikely – lightning doesn't strike twice, and all that – and we were tired of cowering under the stairs. It was a bit of a shock to see that pieces of shrapnel had just torn through the bedroom walls, but at three in the morning you're too tired to think much about such things. We lifted the blankets, shook the glass off them, and prepared to go to sleep. But then the mosquitoes started swarming in through the shattered windows, so we had to go to Salman and Gul's place for the rest of the night. For the rest of the war, in fact, while the house was being patched up.

'But during that night and during the days that followed, I was never frightened at the thought of what had happened. Not for a second. But then, about a week later, when the air-raids seemed to have stopped altogether, Salman and I walked down to Farooq's house for a game of bridge. We had only been playing for about half an hour when the air-raid sirens started up. My hands started shaking, I broke into a cold sweat. It was the first time I hadn't been with you and your mother when the sirens sounded, and I jumped up, tried to run for the door though my knees were jelly, just thinking I had to get to the two of you. Salman grabbed hold of me, and somehow I fell and he fell and the bridge table fell and the glasses on the table fell. I looked down and saw a piece of glass sticking out of my palm. Then I fainted. So, that's how I got the scar. No daring save-the-woman-and-child escapades in my life, I'm afraid.'

At the time Hasan had been disappointed – almost offended, to tell the truth – and was only slightly mollified when Salman Mamoo later added that the glass shard almost went through to Aba's metacarpal and the gush of blood made two bridge-players physically sick. But now, sitting in the car, looking at the scar, he imagined Aba running out on to the street, running towards his family, a perfect bull's-eye for a

43

fighter pilot who could fly low enough to show his razor-cuts. In Hasan's mind the bomb dropped. Dropped on Aba, no, Salman Mamoo, no, Azeem. Hasan rested his head against the car window and envied the girl with the green flecks in her eyes; envied her ability to stand with her fist on her hip and look at him as if nothing in all the world mattered.

Chapter Six

'You can't envy someone a thing like that!'

'Why not?' Hasan said.

Zehra made a sound of exasperation, though whether at Hasan's question or Ogle's inability to respond to the command 'Shake!' it was hard to tell.

'Because. When you're my age you'll understand these things better.'

Hasan laughed, and rolled over on his back in the grass. 'A whole twenty-five months! I can't wait.' The grey boundary wall around Zehra's house didn't seem as stunted as it had yesterday evening when Hasan returned from Salman Mamoo's. Hasan closed his eyes and decided that if he could remain this way long enough for his eyelashes to grow and weave together, Zehra's double-storied, sloping red roofed, multi-balconied house would transform into Salman Mamoo's single-storied, arched-doorwayed, multi-verandahed one. Seconds drifted past. Suddenly the windblown whiffs of Uncle Latif's prized *chikoo* trees dissolved in a concentration of pine smell. 'It worked,' Hasan cried out, his eyelashes springing apart. But the only thing different was Uncle Latif's presence in the driveway, his thumb pumping an air-freshener spray. Hasan closed his eyes again and reached one hand up in the air.

'Still trying to touch the sky?' Zehra said.

'Not really. It's just habit now. Zehra, do you ever wish you could do something?'

'Well, there are some things I wish I could do. Like tap dance.'

'No, I mean really do something. Like in books. Something heroic. Like knights.'

'I'm a pacifist with breasts,' Zehra said archly. 'That counts me out of the Round Table.'

'Zehra!' Hasan turned red, and looked away from her.

'But I think I would have felt the same way, though for different reasons.'

Having a conversation with Zehra was like juggling oranges in the air, never knowing which would land in your palm, or whether they would still be oranges when they landed. Sometimes the oranges would take whole weeks to land, and Hasan would almost forget that they had been left hovering in the air until Zehra would break into a conversation about, say, angels, to comment, 'It might be true for elephants, though.'

Hasan looked back at her, and twirled his fingers in a silent question-mark.

'The girl you saw on the road yesterday,' Zehra said. 'I would have envied her for being able to leave home and walk through the streets. You have to be male or poor to do that.'

Hasan smiled smugly. 'Bet you wish you were a boy, huh?'

'Are you mental! No more than I wish I was poor.'

'God, I can't imagine being a girl. I mean, all the things you can't do. Stupid things. Like . . .'

'. . . wandering around on the roof where everyone can see you.'

Hasan hid his face in Ogle's flank. He could feel Ogle's heartbeat as he ran his fingers over the ridges of the puppy's ribcage, the black fur ruffling against his fingertips: dhuDHUD . . . dhuDHUD . . . Like gunfire. Like the boy's name.

'Azeem,' Zehra said. 'You're thinking about him.'

The time it took him to fall from roof to ground seemed an eternity, longer and longer each time Hasan replayed it in his mind; so long it seemed that if Hasan had just tried, just jumped and run with arms outstretched he could have caught the boy before . . .

'Whenever you talk about it, you talk about the time he was in the air, never about the moment when he actually . . .'

'I don't remember that part.'

'Knobble-knees, this is me you're talking to.' Zehra's voice was very gentle. Hasan almost preferred the moodiness and curtness he had come to expect of her these past few months.

'I don't remember that part,' he insisted. 'It's as if I'm watching a movie, and I'm also in the movie, and I can see him falling in slow motion, and he falls and falls and I see the grass just beneath him, and then I look up and see the kite. I don't even know if I ever saw him . . . you know . . .'

So sometimes he believed it didn't really happen; believed a pair of arms did catch Azeem, and that one day Azeem would walk up to him and say, 'I did it. I flew.'

'You never say the word.'

'What word?'

47

'The word you always replace with 'you know'. And you always cut me off before I can say it, too.'

'Do you ever think about it?'

Zehra leaned back among the fallen almond-shaped berries of the *karonda* trees and ran her fingers through her long, dark hair – her most precious inheritance from her mother, Uncle Latif always said.

'Stupid question,' Hasan muttered. 'Sorry.'

The silence between them lengthened, stretched taut. Like a giant mass of bubble-gum, Hasan thought, and it was impossible to know how to rip through it without the gum splattering on both their faces. Zehra turned her face away, picked up a *karonda* and bit into its purple over-ripeness.

'Zehra?'

Zehra turned around and bared teeth dripping with thick red liquid. 'Blood!' she howled, in an attempt to approximate the voice of the Queen of Drama who had eaten her enemy's liver on television the night before, in the stunning climax of a serial that was almost cancelled because the villain looked remarkably like the President (the villain shaved his presidential moustache and the show was allowed to go on, largely because the President was as big a fan of it as anyone). Ogle leapt up, barking wildly, and spun around in the air. 'Blood!' Zehra shrieked again, but by now the shriek had become one of laughter at Hasan and Ogle entangled in the grass. Hasan saw her raise a bursting *karonda* above his face, felt the juice trickling down his cheek, and yelled as Ogle's tongue darted forward.

'Zehra!' The Widow called out from the balcony upstairs. 'I'm going to sleep. If anyone calls, say I'm falling in love.'

'Okay, Wid.'

'How do you think she would feel if we started calling her "Doe" instead?' Hasan said, wiping Ogle's saliva off his face.

'She isn't very doe-like,' Zehra laughed. 'But I don't suppose she would mind. Do you ever mind, or even remember, what people in your dreams call you?'

Hasan looked up at the balcony. The spot where the Widow had stood still shimmered with the bright greens and yellows of her sari, and the flames of her hennaed hair. A far cry from the day she entered Zehra's house, Hasan recalled, just over three years ago.

It had been winter then, or rather, the City's version of winter, and Hasan stood in Zehra's driveway breathing out great puffs of air. He was so caught up with the two-weeks-of-the-year joy of watching his breath freeze that he didn't hear the taxi draw up outside or notice a woman pushing the side gate open. His breath wisped away and in its place, as though conjured up from the trailing clouds of his own exhalation, stood the Widow.

Her hair was smoke, grey and wafting. Or, at least, it was when Hasan remembered the moment, though Zehra said white and pulled back in a bun. But they both agreed that she was wearing such drab clothes that the chameleon that skittered past on the wall behind her did not need to change its colour to meld in with her apparel. And they both remembered the pillow in her hand.

Zehra had stepped forward. 'Are you the wife of . . .'

'No, the Widow.'

Uncle Latif yelled down from the balcony, '*Bhabi*, don't leave or grieve, I'll be right down.'

'*Bhabi*?' Hasan said to Zehra. 'She's Uncle Latif's brother's wife?'

'Widow,' the woman replied. 'I am the Widow.'

'Not brother's wife,' Zehra hissed back at Hasan, 'Cousin's wife.'

49

The woman raised an eyebrow. 'Sorry,' Zehra said. 'She's the Widow.'

'*Bhabi, bhabi, bhabi*,' Uncle Latif called out, wagging his head with joy as he skipped down the front steps. As ever, his belly seemed to be guiding and propelling the rest of his body along while the breeze tried to carry his shoulder-length, thinning hair in the opposite direction. 'You should have told us when your flight was zooming in, and we would have been standing on the tarmac with garlands to receive you.'

'I know,' the Widow said.

Uncle Latif chuckled and handed her a hibiscus flower. 'Well, this will do. Where are your things?'

The Widow held up her feather pillow. 'This is all they let me take.'

'Good, good, good,' Uncle Latif beamed. 'Perfect excuse to shop till you drop.'

'I don't like shopping.'

'Ah, but I love it, so you must indulge me. We will O-M-I-T the dropping part, though. But tea first. The liquid, not the letter of the alphabet. Hasan go and tell your parents to come over and meet their new neighbour.'

'Neighbour?' Hasan said, following Zehra over the wall between their two houses.

'Her husband died a few days ago. All his brothers came and took everything that belonged to him, even the house – they said it was the law. Aba heard about it, and told her she could come and live here. He didn't say so, but I know he thinks I need a female relative around. I don't really know her. She hasn't been to the City since my mother died. They were very close.' Zehra bounded up the step to Hasan's front door and peered at the surrounding creeper-covered brick wall. Sometimes Hasan wondered if Zehra would ever recover from having a lizard leap on to her hand last year as she turned the door-handle.

'She seems strange,' Hasan said, pushing past Zehra and opening the door.

'I like her. She reminds me of my mother. What's so strange about her?'

'The feather pillow.'

Zehra shrugged then, but an hour past bedtime she ran around to Hasan's garden and knocked on his window. 'You may have been right. Maybe the feather pillow does prove she's strange.'

'Why?'

'Her husband had just bought the pillow when his heart stopped in the doorway of the pillow store. It was the only thing of his that her husband's brothers let her take when they told her to leave the house.'

'Oh,' Hasan said. 'That's not so strange. It would be strange if she was carrying it around just like that, no slime or season.'

The next morning the Widow announced that she had dreamed of her husband while she slept, and then again the next morning and the next and the next. Each of those mornings she awoke to find a feather from her pillow curled around her wedding ring. The fifth night a soreness in her neck prompted her to sleep pillowless, and she did not dream at all. Hasan was having breakfast with Zehra and Uncle Latif the morning after the fifth night, when the Widow swept out on to the verandah to announce she knew what was going on: every feather in the pillow was a dream about her husband.

Or rather, each feather was a chapter of a dream, for there was a clear chronology that connected each dream; a chronology not of time but of love. Yes, the Widow declared, after thirteen years of marriage she was falling in love with her husband, and he with her. The growing intensity of their love was manifested in the increasing brightness of the colours of her dreams, which had once been black and white. By the end of her first month at Zehra's house the Widow's dreams had become so bright the waking world seemed drab by comparison and she had to swathe herself in clothes of bright greens and reds and yellows so that she would not see greyness every time she passed by a mirror.

She treated the waking world like a dream which has revealed its unreality, and for the most part she would participate in it with amusement, even suspicion at its illogic, but always with an air of remove, always waiting for her eyelids to droop and the real work of living to begin.

But there were always those moments when she would suddenly snap her neck up, open her eyes wide, lean out of the nearest window and sniff at the air. 'Smell it,' she would say, 'Sorrow and greed.' Then she would walk out of the house and sometimes disappear for days.

In less than a year she was legend, and whenever Mrs Ahmed seemed poised to announce weekend homework Hasan would distract her with tales of the latest trail of sorrow and greed that led the Widow to a house of mourning.

'And were the brothers of the deceased about to convince their sister-in-law that the law entitled them to all her husband's property?' Mrs Ahmed would demand.

'Oh yes, miss,' Hasan would reply. 'But the Widow got there just in time and quoted the inheritance laws loud enough for all the mourners to hear, and then she chased the brothers away with quotes from the Quran and the Hadith about honouring widows and safeguarding the rights of your widowed sisters-in-law.'

'Ha!' Mrs Ahmed would say, and the students' homework diaries stayed blank.

Hasan lay among the *karondas* and laughed at the memory of Mrs Ahmed stabbing the air in triumph with her fist while everyone in the class gave Hasan smiles of the deepest gratitude. And then he remembered what the Widow had said when Hasan asked her what would happen when she had dreamed every feather in her pillow.

She said, 'I will die.'

Chapter Seven

Generally speaking, though, the Widow was hale and vigorous enough to remove all urgency from Hasan's and Zehra's attempts to count the number of feathers in clandestinely purchased pillows of the same brand as the Widow's pillow. It was only on those days when death-threats arrived that the counting and calculations took place in earnest behind locked doors.

'She's been here . . .' Zehra would purse her lips, consult calculator and calendar, and write down how many days it had been since the Widow started dreaming, while Hasan rent open a pillow with his penknife.

The first moment was always the most satisfying; Hasan dipped his hand into the mass of feathers and scooped out a handful, recalling the feel of new-born chicks stirring in his hand. But after that it was sweat and sneezing until the tedium of the counting became too much to bear and Hasan and Zehra decided yes, no question about it, obvious at a glance that the feathers numbered far more than the dreams, so the Widow would live for a while yet. Besides, not infrequently the threats to reunite the Widow with her dead husband turned out merely to be advertisements for the services of spiritualists. Consequently, all the threats were tinged with the possibility of farce, and only occasionally did Hasan imagine that some moustachioed man walking towards Zehra's house was really an irate brother to a corpse, come to kill the woman who had cheated him out of his illegal share of inheritance. Frankly, though he never said so, Hasan was grateful for the death-threats, for without them the Bodyguard would never have come into being.

Even now, after all this time, Hasan knew very little about the Bodyguard, except that it had appeared – in the form of three women and a boy – the day the first death-threat arrived. When Uncle Latif demanded to know why the four strangers were sitting in the patch of lawn just outside his house, the eldest woman replied, in village dialect, 'Because you have not invited us in yet.'

Uncle Latif's hospitality opened his mouth to invite the four in, but his social snobbery and City-dweller suspicion of strangers constricted his voice box, so he could only gape.

'Don't bother,' the youngest woman said. 'We can guard her better if we keep watch outside.'

'Her?'

'The Widow.'

The next day they were gone, but a group of five was in their place. Thereafter, the Bodyguard changed character daily, and it became a morning tradition for Hasan and Zehra to sing out a description of its latest composition to the Widow:

'One old woman, toothless
Her daughter you did save.
By her side her grandson
He must be Hasan's age.'

Or:

'Five women, three men, one in between
Plus the largest rooster we've ever seen
They don't know each other, yet here they are
'Cause of the Wid, 'bout whom they rave "wah wah!"'

The Widow merely smiled her off-centred smile that could
have been directed anywhere, and ordered Imran to see to it
that the visitors were given food and water. The first time she
said this Uncle Latif almost choked on his tea. Imran's culinary
excellence was matched only by his snobbery, and when he
had first come to work for Uncle Latif he claimed to have quit
his previous job because his ex-employees were given to dis-
playing their newly acquired wealth by sprinkling fistfuls of
saffron on every dish he made. Saffron aside, Imran had said,
the company of people lacking class invariably made his food
taste bitter. But though the Widow's instructions drained the
colour from his face, he did as she asked. Before long, Imran's
expression of stoic forbearance as he counted the number of
the Bodyguard was as much a part of the morning ritual as
were Hasan and Zehra's rhymes.

But other than making sure they were fed, the Widow never
acknowledged the Bodyguard's existence, even when its var-
iegated numbers followed on her heels through crowded
bazaars, houses of mourning and the law library (where,
according to Mansoor of the Bodyguard, the Widow was only

admitted because one of the security guards at the library was Mansoor's uncle's brother's wife's nephew's cousin. 'You mean he's your cousin,' Zehra said. 'My brother,' said Mansoor. Hasan was so awed by Mansoor's ability to complicate the relationship that he never mentioned that actually it was Aba's intercession with the Library Board that gave the Widow access to the library).

At any rate, despite the City's initial murmurs of disapproval ('My dear, that rabble makes one afraid to approach her on the streets'), skepticism ('They're just doing it for the free food') and whispered curiosity ('Do you suppose they follow her into the bath?'), not to mention all the 'Not to spread rumours, but I've heard . . .' stories, within a year of its inception the Bodyguard's position altered from gawk-and-talk-of-the-town to bemusing-but-amusing-institution. And in the last few months, as violence in the City spread even to its more élite enclaves, the Bodyguard had become a source of envy among the many women who found themselves paying for the services of armed bodyguards who terrified them. But it was only on the day of Uncle Latif's annual party, less than two weeks after mid-term ended, that the last bastion of resistance to the Bodyguard crumbled.

'It's happened. It's finally happened,' Zehra announced, bounding into Hasan's room. 'Oh, are you still pouting?' Hasan was. 'Can you at least tell me why?'

Why should have been obvious. For the last few days Zehra had been spending hours on the phone with Najam, Hasan's cousin with the one-haired chest, and in school she tilted her head to one side and tucked strands of hair behind her left ear whenever Najam was around. All this was inexcusable enough, but today when Najam had demanded to know why

Zehra spent so much time at Hasan's house, Zehra replied, 'Oh, you know how it is. He's my neighbour.'

'Well, you are my neighbour,' Zehra said, when Hasan revealed his complaint. Hasan turned his face from her and pretended to gaze, enrapt, at the mural of the Milky Way which Ami had painted on one of his walls. During the day the mural showed the creatures of the constellations – Bear, Lion, Hunter, Crab, and the like – circling each other, each claw, bristle and nail delineated; but at night, when darkness swallowed up detail, scattered smudges of luminous paint made stars glow on the wall.

Zehra poked Hasan in the ribs. 'No more head-tilting, okay? Solemn vow. Now, listen . . . Imran has accepted the Bodyguard.'

Hasan fell on his knees beside his bed and made scraping gestures on the carpet. 'Keep going,' he said. 'I'm just picking up my jaw.'

'To put it in an eggshell, Imran got into yet another fight with your new no-name cook, and while arguing forgot to tend to the chicken he was cooking, and it burned. So, minor crisis happened. Then your cook said he was quitting and stormed out of the house, attempting to take your mother's silver with him, but the Bodyguard stopped him and recovered the goods.'

'That made Imran accept the Bodyguard after three years of complaining about having to cook for them?'

'Not at all. We only reached the minor crisis. Imran then pedalled off to the market to buy more chickens but . . . it's a meatless day. No flesh or fowl available, except the frozen variety which, of course, Imran refuses to cook. So, major calamity. Much wailing, hair-pulling, contemplation of suicide from Imran, which flung my father into a panic, which in turn really upset Ogle who tried to chew the Widow's pillow as an outlet for all his disorientation, which really woke the Widow up for once, which made the Bodyguard take things in their own hands.' Zehra fell back gasping, and in a final burst spurted out: 'So a bunch of them disappeared somewhere and returned in half an hour with no less than eight chickens.'

'Were they fresh?' Hasan asked.

'Very. They were alive.'

There was always some crisis or another to contend with in the hours leading up to Uncle Latif's annual party, and Imran was usually at the centre of it. But from the moment Khan, son of Khan, unofficial leader of the Bodyguard, plugged in the outdoor lights that nestled between branches of the *chikoo* trees some angel with a taste for panache and Imran's stuffed green chillies took over.

Hasan and Zehra stood on the Widow's balcony, which overlooked the shorter stem of the L-shaped garden, and watched the visible patches of grass shrink further and further as the evening progressed. 'We're on Olympus. I'm Aphrodite – no, Artemis – and you're Hermes, and we have to decide whether to exterminate the human race or not based on this party,' Zehra said.

Hasan kicked up his heels to indicate winged sandals and scrutinized the proceedings with the eyes of an impartial god. The buds of *Raat-ki-rani* had opened wider than usual tonight and their scent mingled with women's perfume and men's cologne; the lights from the *chikoo* tree illuminated the reddest hibiscus, the whitest *motia*, the greenest leaf. Not one flower drooped in the centre-pieces of the eight round tables and nocturnal birds resisted the temptation to soil the white tablecloths. Cigarette butts and mosquito coils glowed; Club bearers slipped from group to group holding aloft silver salvers laden with illegal beverages; no one's heels sank into damp mud.

The men were disappointments as usual – a dark-suited bunch, lightly smattered with *shalwar kameezes* made formal by the addition of waistcoats with high collars. At least Aba's silk cravat acquired him some distinction, though he had only worn it at Ami's insistence. So much for the men. But the women! *Saris*, *peshwazes*, *sheraras*, sleeveless *kameezes* and some garbs that even Zehra couldn't name. It was no surprise that Ami preferred painting women, Hasan thought. But he wondered if even Ami's palette was capable of reproducing all the colours arrayed on the lawn.

'Your mother's the most beautiful woman here,' Zehra said. She stood on tip-toes, though she had outgrown the balcony railing some years ago. Hasan nodded. Ami had surveyed herself earlier in the evening and laughed that she would look like a crow among Birds of Paradise, but as she waved up at the balcony Hasan found himself standing a little taller and moving his face into the light so that anyone who looked up would know he was her son.

She was wearing something new. '*Angarkha*,' Zehra said. 'Originally a man's coat, but you lot didn't appreciate it enough so we adapted it.' Ami's *angarkha*, worn over a *shalwar*, was black and fell to mid-calf. Gold paisleys bordered by gold piping made a dramatic hem and played off against the gold and emerald choker around Ami's throat. She had brushed her hair off her face and her cheekbones challenged gravity.

'Admit, admit, o vision in green!' Uncle Latif appeared beneath the balcony, resplendent in raw silk *sherwani*, and held out his arms towards the Widow. He had shifted the excess pounds from his stomach on to his chest and the effort made his voice choke. 'Eat your words without salt. This is grander than grand, eh? More okay than dokay?'

The Widow laughed and took his arm. 'Yes, and I'm sure Nero was an excellent fiddler. By the way, did you know you're compromising my honour by not marrying me? One of your friends just told me so.'

'Take me to this friend! Let me say, "I've tried to compromise her, but she just won't allow it".'

Zehra refused to explain what Uncle Latif meant, which proved she didn't know herself and was just looking amused to disguise her ignorance. 'Come on,' she said, when Hasan tried to catch her out. 'It's time for dinner.' She raced to her own balcony with the speed that had once prompted Uncle Latif to tell her to slow down for modesty's sake lest her clothes fail to keep up with her.

Zehra's balcony looked down on the longer, slimmer part of the garden where *chikoo* trees gave way to squat shrubs that did not impede wall-climbing. The Bodyguard had placed five wooden tables end to end in the garden, their splintered ricketiness concealed beneath a starched white tablecloth. Five brass warming-pans glowed above spirit-lamps. Further back in the garden, earthenware bowls of *kheer* were paired together, one covering the other to keep the flies away. It was a mark of well set *kheer* that when the bearers separated the bowls like musicians unclashing cymbals not a speck of *kheer* would dislodge. But before that could happen, there was the main course to attend to.

Uncle Latif signalled five bearers who each placed a hand on the covers of the warming-pans and, as one, raised the lids. There was no need to announce that dinner was served – the aroma was dinner-gong enough. There was *pulao* with peas nestling in the rice; prawn *vindaloo* which made Hasan's eyes stream and throat burn just from looking at it; *murgh mussalum* made with such tender pieces of chicken that Imran was seen hugging three members of the Bodyguard after he sampled it; fried okra, crisped to crunchiness; and, of course, the ultimate medley of meat, onion and spices – Imran's *kharay masalay ki korma*. At the end of the table a basket of *na'an* was surrounded by various *achaars*, chutneys and the delicacy which Aba claimed Shakespeare had foretold: 'Such stuffed chillies as dreams are made on.'

Businessmen, artists, army officers and journalists clinked glasses together in honour of appetite; estranged couples shared bowls of *kheer*; Ami and Aba danced together after the music stopped playing.

'Oh, Artemis,' Hasan whispered. 'Let them live.'

Chapter Eight

'*Skal ego com par tram du sumer's daeg.*'

Hasan frowned as he heard Aba's voice drift across the garden. When Aba started translating lines of poetry into their root words it was clear something was worrying him; but when the poetry was Shakespeare's sonnets . . .

'Bad. Badder than bad,' Uncle Latif whispered to Hasan, wagging his head from side to side. 'Under General Circumstances he's calm by Sonnet Six, but here we must have Major Circumstance which has propelled him to Sonnet Eighteen with no sign of brakes coming into effect. I think I will crawl back to my side of the wall until called for.'

For a moment Hasan was tempted to follow Uncle Latif's loping stride out of the gate, but something in the hunch of Aba's shoulder changed his mind.

'*Swa lang lifian this and this gefan lif to tram.*' Aba slapped a twig against his thigh as he paced up and down the garden.

'Aba?'

'Huss!' Aba came to a stop and rocked back and forth on his heels. 'How was the match? And how did you get that?' Aba ran the twig along the chlorophyll mark that stained Hasan's white trousers from thigh to shin.

'We won. I scored fifty-three. Clean bowled at the end. And I took an incredible diving catch. At mid-wicket. The stain is my souvenir. I'll never wash these trousers. What's bothering you?'

'Well, I couldn't remember the rhyming couplet in Sonnet Eleven. That's a little discomforting. Plus, you've suddenly adopted a speech pattern that resembles bursts of machine-gun fire. And if all this wasn't enough, my wife is in her studio trying to convince two of the most influential men in the art world that they should exhibit her paintings internationally. They've been in there nearly an hour now and the suspense is driving me ga-ga.'

'Deep breaths,' Hasan suggested. 'I thought they weren't coming until tomorrow.'

Aba looked pained. 'We all thought that. So your mother went off shopping and suddenly the bell rang and there they were. And I had to entertain them.' Aba's look of horror suggested that waltzing with a rhinoceros might have been a more soothing way of spending his evening. 'God knows how I managed. But I think I did a pretty good job, talking about this and that, everything and nothing.

'You mean MVG?'

'What?'

'Male Vacuous Garrulousness. Gul Mumani told me all about it.'

There was no one in the world with a laugh as infectious as Aba's. It started as a booming sound – the rapid beating of a drum – meshed with the growl of a revving motorcycle

64

engine, and finally melded into the swoosh! of palm-leaves slapping together in a monsoon shower. When the three sounds achieved a crescendo their contagion was so great even the lilies dropped their posture of indifferent elegance and swayed from side to side, and the voice of the muezzin cracked over the loudspeaker as he called the faithful to prayer. Hasan usually prayed at *maghrib*, brought to his knees in adulation by the sunset, but today the laughter seemed worship enough. He could almost, oh-so-nearly, see his own laughter rising up in the air, riding on the backs of Aba's three laughs as they spiralled around the day's last shaft of sunlight.

'Do you always have so much fun while I'm not around?'

Ami stood in the driveway – alone – arms akimbo in mock authority. Peter Pan, Hasan thought, marking her posture and the green of her *kameez*. Leader of Lost Boys.

'What happened? Where are they?' Aba said.

'They just left.' She grinned and flung out her arms. 'They love my stuff!' Aba whooped with joy and swung her around in his arms. Hasan found it a little hard to be quite so enthusiastic about the inevitable but he succumbed to the impulse to turn cartwheels.

'How shall we celebrate?' Aba said.

'Tea,' said Ami.

What were those words Salman Mamoo had sung to Ami last year when she refused to wake up in time for a sunrise hike? *We savoured the dew, wrapped tongues round the mist/Now your taste-buds mainly crave tea, dear sis.*

'Everything A-okay?' Uncle Latif yelled down from his balcony.

'Better than A-okay,' Ami yelled back. 'Come over for dinner later and we'll tell you.'

65

'Ho, Shehryar!' Uncle Latif said. 'What's the etymology of "etymology"?'

'From the Greek *etymos* meaning "true", akin to *eteos* which also means "true", which comes from the Latin *esse* meaning "to be",' Aba shouted back. 'Why are you pretending to be interested?'

Uncle Latif held up his massive red dictionary. 'Because I already looked it up. From *esse* meaning "to be"! So in his solo-liliquy Hamlet was saying "Etymology or not etymology". Finally the light, the light. This is why he's your favourite literary character.'

The new cook – Atif? Asif? Arif? – brought three cups of tea and a box of wheat biscuits into the TV room. Ami and Aba sang between sips, inventing lyrics to old tunes, inventing dance steps to old lyrics. Aba stepped on Ami's foot mid-twirl and she responded by biting his knuckle.

'You've been spending too much time at the office,' Ami said. 'You taste of paper.'

Ami wasn't usually given to such careless remarks. Referring to the taste of paper was a little like referring to the taste of chicken, as though there weren't hundreds of levels of fowl taste ranging from Imran's chicken *korma* to Farah Khala's half-raw chicken in ketchup that wasn't palatable even when she called it p*oulet avec tomatre.*

Last year, Nargis Lotia had acquired sudden glory when her uncle returned from overseas with a diary for Nargis that had both combination lock and key lock. Nargis wouldn't let anyone see inside the diary, even though she hadn't started writing in it yet, but she did tear out the middle page and pass it around the class. The paper was so smooth and thick and creamy that Hasan couldn't resist tearing off a corner and putting it in his mouth. After that, everyone wanted a taste and Nargis was forced to rip out another page. Hasan tasted the paper again in his mouth, its corner cutting his tongue like a particularly sour lemon. It was hard to imagine Aba's knuckle tasting anything like that. Too bony.

'What does Aba usually taste like?' Hasan asked. 'When he's not at the office so much?'

'Sea-air,' Ami smiled. 'With the slightest hint of crab.' She touched Aba at the place where his neck met his shoulder. 'Especially right there.' Hasan wanted to ask Ami why she knew such a strange piece of information, but she and Aba were dancing again.

Hasan slid his fingers along the face of his cricket bat. It was slightly bowed in the centre, testimony to Hasan's gift for repeatedly striking the ball with the centre of his bat to produce the most wonderful sound in the world: Thock! Thock! Thock! Thock! Hasan recalled his afternoon innings. Thock! Aba was laughing again. Hasan closed his eyes and froze the moment. On a day like this even shin burns were sources of delight.

Outside the gate a car horn beeped peh-peh-pehpehpeh.

Salman Mamoo's code!

Hasan charged towards the open window, and slid out from under the grilles. His shoulder caught against one pointed grille in his haste, but he barely noticed the tear of fabric and skin. He could hear Ami and Aba running out through the door, and he permitted himself a momentary smile at his own litheness and agility. Hasan dropped down on the ground, off-balanced on to his hands and knees, picked himself up and rounded the corner into the driveway at the same time as Ami and Aba ran out through the front door and Atif-Asif-Arif flung open the gate.

Only Gul Mumani was in the car.

She hurtled into the driveway, screeched to a halt, threw the handbrake and, with the ignition still running, she half-fell out of the car and into Ami and Aba's arms, weeping.

'They've taken him away. They've taken Salman to prison.'

Chapter Nine

At first Gul Mumani's words didn't mean anything. At least, they didn't mean anything they should have. Hasan heard 'prism' for 'prison' and pictured Salman Mamoo sitting cross-legged in a glass room, capturing light in cupped palms and sifting it through his fingers into rainbow colours. But then Hasan looked across the bonnet of the car and something in Ami's and Aba's faces made him think, 'Some day one of them will die, and I will have to look after the other one.'

'Prison?' Ami said, and Hasan was grateful to have something else to think about.

Gul Mumani was sobbing and trying to dry her tears on Aba's sleeve at the same time. Prison, Hasan said to himself. Prison. The word sank down to his stomach, cold and smooth.

Ami put an arm around Gul Mumani's shoulders and led her into the house. Gul Mumani seemed barely aware of what was happening and kept repeating a single phrase over and over. The words disappeared and became a rhythm that was echoed in the throb of her Corolla's engine and the mating call of birds. Tu-whit-to-woo. What will they do?

Aba's brown eyes were suddenly hazel, as though shock had stripped away a layer of colouring. 'They won't do anything,' he said patting Hasan's shoulder. The gesture should have been comforting but Hasan couldn't help feeling that Aba wanted to reassure himself that Hasan was still there. 'They won't do anything,' Aba repeated, his hand capping Hasan's head. 'Don't be afraid.'

I'm not, Hasan nearly said. He wasn't quite sure what he was feeling, but it had nothing of the intensity of panic he was used to experiencing when a ball smacked off his bat and climbed in the air, giving a fielder ample time to get under it before it descended.

In the TV room, Gul Mumani was holding up a vanity case and wiping away smudges of mascara from her face with a tissue. She closed the case with a snap and made a final dab near her eye which left a curve of mascara smeared across her cheek. The smear was located beneath two moles. Hasan fingered the yellow and black markers on the side table and considered drawing a Smiley on Gul Mumani's cheek. Ami put out an arm and drew him close.

'I knew it as soon as I woke up yesterday, six am, up before next-door's rooster even,' Gul Mumani said. 'My eyes just popped open and I looked at the clock and thought, that's strange, because (a) what kind of hour is that to wake up? and (b) I couldn't remember what I had been dreaming of, and Sai, you know that's not normal for me, although all right such a thing isn't necessarily whatchamacallit, portentous.' Gul Mumani paused to light a cigarette. She did not take a puff, but held the tip just inches from her face and inhaled through her nose. The smoke-scent combined with her rose-scent to create the odour of decaying wreaths.

'So I went outside because I couldn't go back to sleep and I didn't want to wake up Saloo. I was walking around the garden and I heard the guards outside, well, didn't hear what they were saying exactly, but heard the tone of their voices and I can't tell you, I felt a fear, not just fear, but *a* fear, one particular variety, like the kind Rustum felt when he bent over the dying soldier he had struck down, the young one, Sohrab, and Sohrab said, "My father will kill you for this. My father, Rustum." That fear – the one that knows you will undo the dead soldier's collar and find there the locket you sent to your child whom you haven't seen all these years. That fear. I ran inside and shook Saloo awake. You know what he's usually like – he's like you, Shehryar; tells me my imagination is running a marathon. But not this time. He came outside with me, and he felt it too.

'Maybe he knew right away. It's possible, because straight away he said, let's call Saira, just to chat, and I said, *baba*, she's in the same time-zone as you are, you can't phone at this o'clock. But he picked up the phone and without dialling said, oh yes, you're right. Too early. What was I thinking? Let's cook breakfast. Well, Saira, you know the last time your brother acted so nonchalant a bomb had just missed blowing him up, so I picked up the phone and it was dead.

'Well, what to do? Salman just said, oh it means nothing. Phones are forever dysfunctional. So we're in the kitchen, it's Zahoor's day off, making breakfast and a guard – the really courteous one with the amazing jaw, you know? – appears and says we're not to step outside, can't even go in the garden . . .'

'What did Salman Mamoo do?'

'He offered the man a fried egg. The guard said, no thank

you, I have high cholesterol.' She inhaled cigarette smoke once more and let out a sound that was half-sigh, half-laugh. 'The rest of the day went so slowly it made seven-hour lay-overs in airports seem double-speed in comparison. We couldn't understand whats or whys, and neither of us was willing to really talk because if we did we knew the word 'assassination' would pop out. But I was thinking it, thinking it until my toes curled and wouldn't uncurl, until Salman said, look if they wanted to get rid of me they'd just do it. No shilly-shallying.

'So six o'clock the pine-cones fell and it was the first day since this whole thing started that Salman hadn't stood outside watching them hail around him. He started to go crazy, you know, pacing around our bedroom, muttering to himself. I couldn't hear what he was saying but I was afraid it was terrible and the wire-taps would pick it up so I said shut up, Saloo, shut up, and there we were yelling at each other when the garden sweeper threw a pine-cone in through the window. Salman calmed down then but as for me, I mean, I appreciate symbolic gestures and all that but I'm happier when one doesn't hit me on the head.' She fished a pine-cone out of her handbag and handed it to Hasan. 'Here, I know you appreciate these more than I do.' Hasan took the pine-cone but what he really wanted was to hug Gul Mumani.

'Then, maybe an hour or hour and a half ago, we heard more vehicles drive up to, and then inside, our gate, and Salman walked out of the front door when he heard them. He told me to stay inside – what sort of John Wayne comment is that! – of course I told him to shut up. Then I followed him out, and in the driveway there were two jeeps with tinted windows, unmarked licence plates. The doors of both jeeps opened and out came six men, military men, with guns, though not thank God! pointed at us, just visible so we would know. They walked up to Salman and he saluted them. Will someone explain that to me? I was about to spit at them. I mean, execute the messengers I say, if they agree to carry the message. But they saluted in return, which surprised me, and one said, "I'm going to have to ask you sir, to come with us." I thought they were a firing squad.'

In the pause that followed, filled only by the sound of Gul Mumani striking a match against flint with such vigour the match head snapped off, Hasan could not look up. He gripped the pine-cone, but though his palm was marked with dozens of crescents he felt nothing.

'For a moment I went mad,' Gul Mumani continued. 'Actually, truly mad. It was as though everything in my brain got pushed back, what's the word? compressed against my skull, and in the centre of my brain there was just blinding light. Maybe a doctor would argue – neurons, cerebellum, medulla oblongata whatever – but I know. Blinding light. The only way to shut it out, fill it up, was cry, kick, scream. I did. I even kicked Salman.

'I think I would have gone on and on until I dropped from exhaustion if it hadn't been for one of the army chaps who called me by my name. I was so startled I looked up, saw his face for the first time, and it was Javed. Mona's brother, you know? Who I had a crush on in college. He took me to one side and said, 'We have orders for his arrest. No more. He's going to be tried for treason. A former ACE party worker just made a deathbed confession of a planned coup attempt, and he named your husband as the chief plotter.' Then they led Salman to the jeep, and drove out. They told me I would have to stay at home for an hour – long enough to get Salman safely inside jail – Safely! – and then the guards outside would leave and I would be free to do whatever.

'You know, all the books, stories, movies, they all get it wrong. When you say goodbye to your husband in a moment like that you don't do any of this clasping to your bosom and vowing eternal love-shove, you don't smile bravely and say everything will be all right, you don't break into tears and cling on to him until the guards tear you apart. You just stand and look at him. And when the car drives out your hand raises itself to wave goodbye as though he were just leaving for the supermarket. But then you turn to go inside, see the door-frame which he used to lean against while watching you come and go, and you close your eyes, wrap your arms around the place where his torso used to be and rest your head against his imagined shoulder.'

Gul Mumani curled herself up on the sofa. 'He didn't even have any lunch. I hope they feed him properly.'

'You know he has a tiny appetite,' Ami said. This seemed to bring Gul Mumani some relief, because she nodded and fell asleep.

Hasan waited for Aba to crack a joke or Ami to run spider-fingers up his arm until he laughed himself on to the floor, but Aba's hands were blinkers on the side of his face and Ami's arms were holding her body together.

'He'll be all right,' Hasan said. And then, in a rhetorical move Aba often used to reduce all crises to mundanity, Hasan added, 'What's the worst that can happen?'

There followed a quiet that reminded Hasan of some movie which used slow-motion and silence to depict a sword slicing through air and flesh and life. The dying man's knees buckled; he crashed to the ground, arms widespread, and before his face came into view there was just enough time to know with a movie-goer's savvy that he was the hero, and then enough time to hope that he was not.

'Quite right,' Aba said, getting to his feet and brushing imaginary crumbs off his shirt. 'At worst he'll develop a taste for prison food and never want to eat Gul's cooking again.'

At the mention of her name, Gul Mumani sat upright and said, 'Ignition!' Hasan envisioned flames.

The door opened and the Widow entered, dangling Gul Mumani's car keys from her fingers. 'I heard,' she said to Aba. 'The Bodyguard told Zehra. They know everything that goes on in the City.' She squeezed Ami's hand; Hasan had never seen her exhibit such intimacy with anyone other than Zehra before. 'Huss, can you come over for dinner? Zehra's a little moody today; she might cheer up if you're around.'

Zehra seemed fine when Hasan saw her a few minutes later. She and Uncle Latif were sitting close to the stereo in their lounge, attempting to decipher lyrics that doubled as dance instructions. The sofas and floor-cushions had been pushed against the wall and the *bukhara* rug was rolled up to one side. Ladies at their toilets in Mughal miniatures cast sidelong looks at princes hunting on the adjacent wall. Zehra seemed to have decided that the key to being a good dancer was shaking one shoulder in time to the music.

'Oh, Hussy, join in,' Uncle Latif said. 'First get one leg a shakin'. No, no Hasan, that's just shaking. We want a-shakin'. A-shakin'. Oh, *yaar*, pathetic. Pa-thetic. Let's face it, daughter and shorter, my generation is *the* generation, you lot are *de* generation. Better. Better. Okay, now we butt butts . . .'

Hasan's stomach muscles were still aching an hour later when he straddled the railing of Zehra's balcony and craned his neck for shooting stars. A massive power-failure through the City – yet another presage of sweltering summer – meant even the most bashful stars had unveiled themselves in the dark. Hasan coaxed the corner of his eye away from the candlelit silhouettes of Ami and Aba which paced across the TV room window, and tried to count the stars which fit between his circled thumb and forefinger when he squinted.

'So is this like a tradition passed on from uncle to nephew in your family?' Zehra said, leaning on the railing. 'Going to prison, I mean.'

Hasan laughed. Sometimes he thought his earliest memory was of Salman Mamoo sitting cross-legged on a floor-cushion and, ignoring Ami's sigh, beginning:

'This is exactly how it happened: Zafar Haq, known to his friends as Zephyr because he was a cool breeze across the arid landscape of politics, awoke one morning in his rain-dripping prison cell and saw the breeze calligraphing "*Azadi*" in the dust of the prison floor. That single word of freedom told Zafar Haq that eight months of imprisonment were over, and he set about moistening his hands with rain and then pressing his *kameez* between his palms to smooth away the creases.

'The rain stopped when he was working on the cuff of his left sleeve, but before Zafar Haq could even think of a suitable word of abuse the prison warden opened his cell door. The courts had cleared him of all charges of corruption and the members of the National Assembly, both government and opposition, had urged bamboozled begged the Prime Minister to set Zafar Haq free.

'Zafar Haq walked out of the prison and the first person he waved to among the throng gathered to greet him was his nephew, eight-year-old Salman. He did not wave to his niece Saira, and she suffered many long lasting personality disorders as a result.' Ami rolled her eyes, but did not interrupt.

'In a playing field just near the prison, a group of boys was playing cricket. One of the boys hit a magnificent six, which flew out of the field, over the heads of the throng and landed at the feet of Zafar Haq. Zafar Haq picked up the ball, whispered something to it, and threw it back to the field. Young Salman, sitting on his father's shoulders, saw that ball spin through the air, over the throng, over long-on, over mid-on, heading straight for silly mid-on, but just as the fielder reached out to catch it, the ball spun out of reach, struck the pitch and broke to dislodge leg-stump. Three months later Zafar Haq was elected Prime Minister.'

Hasan closed his eyes and saw a cricket ball (spinning, spinning) which knocked the President out cold and gathered speed to shatter the bars of Salman Mamoo's cell.

Chapter Ten

Hasan's hand slipped off the mattress and travelled much too short a distance before hitting the carpet. The carpet was marble. Hasan jerked upright, and tried to remember how exactly he had come to fall asleep in Zehra's room. He recalled the balcony and the power-failure; oh, yes, and the electricity returned and Uncle Latif called Hasan and Zehra downstairs to watch a movie . . . and then there was a thumping sound. Uncle Latif's heart against Hasan's ear as Uncle Latif carried Hasan upstairs.

Hasan spun his wrist, glanced down, and leaped off the mattress. 'Zehra,' he yelled. 'It's nearly seven. Wake up!'

Zehra raised her head a few inches off her bed. 'No school . . . strike.' Her head fell back on the pillow and she seemed to say something else, but it was just a snore.

Hasan punched the air in triumph. No Geography test! It occurred to him that Salman Mamoo was probably the reason for the strike. He smiled all the way back to his house. To think, the whole City, the whole entire City, had come to a standstill because of Salman Mamoo. And just two years ago most people said he only won the by-election because the electorate saw his face, heard his voice, and thought they were voting for the ghost of his dead uncle, Zafar. Hasan couldn't wait to see what the papers were saying today.

Ami and Aba's faces ruined Hasan's mood completely. Both of them looked as though they hadn't slept at all; Hasan felt nothing but anger when he looked at them. He slouched down on a sofa and answered Ami's questions about last night in monosyllables. The newspaper hadn't arrived yet. Hasan longed for the ease of Uncle Latif's house and the pleasure of Imran's french toast. He was about to excuse himself when he heard *chapals* slip-slapping against floor and foot floorfoot floorfoot in the hallway.

'Newspaper,' Arif-Atif-Asif announced in the doorway, holding up a rolled-up bundle of black and white. 'The news-paperman says he's sorry it's late, but he has to cover five delivery routes today because even though the newspapermen have been allowed to work through the strike, many of them live in curfew areas and can't work in any case. That's what the newspaperman says, but I think he just overslept this morning.' He handed Ami the paper and slip-slapped a return to the kitchen.

Ami rolled the rubber band off the bundle and the paper sprung open, spewing out sports page, comic strips and cross-word so that only the main paper stayed in Ami's hands. She scanned the front page, frowned; turned to the back page, the frown deepened. Her hands and eyes accelerated, zipped through the inside pages and columns, her fingers darkening with newsprint. She dropped the main paper, sped through the sports page, but nothing uncreased her brow. Finally she looked up, and Aba must have heard her words before they travelled from thought to speech because he was already up and moving towards her, towards the papers she threw down, when she said, 'Not one mention. Not a word. Nothing.'

Now Hasan knew what anger was, and it was not the thing he had felt when seeing Ami and Aba's expressions. This was anger: the memory of Salman Mamoo taking seven hours to drive from the airport to his house the day after he resigned from the government and called for a no-confidence motion; seven hours, because the people, so many people it seemed each one of the City's ten million inhabitants were out in the streets calling out his name, shouting out his last name, 'Haq! Haq!', until it was both a call to him and a call for him to become his name, to become Haq, become justice; seven hours, because the people were dancing, God! dancing and cheering and blowing whistles in the street, despite the police who still tended to incline their heads at Salman Mamoo because it was only twenty-four hours since he was a government minister and perhaps soon he would be even more, so for now the police did not disperse the crowd with tear-gas or bring down their batons on spine and neck and anything else that came in the way, and perhaps they abstained also because they were part of the people too though they could not say it and could barely even think it, and Salman Mamoo pulled Hasan up to peer out of the sunroof with him and wave to the crowd, and the next day Hasan was newsprint, front page, waving by Salman Mamoo's side under banner headlines which proclaimed Salman Mamoo the saviour, the future, the only hope. This was anger: discovering that, less than five months later, Salman Mamoo's imprisonment didn't even get a page six side-bar.

Hasan returned from memory at the sound of Aba using a word he never used.

'What is it, Shehryar?' Ami asked.

'Did you see the headline?' Aba said.

Ami leaned against Aba's arm and looked down at the paper in his tightly clenched fists. '"President signs historic treaty",' she read out loud. She shrugged. 'All the treaties he signs are historic. After all, he commissions the writing of the history books.' But then she read more and her face took on a kind of bafflement that Hasan was used to seeing on his four-year-old cousin's face. 'This doesn't make sense,' she said. 'He'll bankrupt the nation. And for what?' Her lips turned grey. 'Dear God, no,' she said

'What?' Hasan said. 'What?'

Aba and Ami looked up, as though they had just remembered that he existed. They exchanged glances, and Ami unclasped her hands and spread them wide, before letting them fall to her lap. 'Unless you have a glass bubble hidden away, we had better tell him,' she said.

Aba beckoned Hasan over to come and sit beside him. 'I'm sorry,' he said. 'Eleven is too young for this.' Hasan squirmed away from Aba, but Ami caught his hand and pulled him down. Leaning into the curve of her body, Hasan felt he could bear anything.

'You know, Huss, whenever we talked about Salman Mamoo and what would happen to him, we were always sure that he would not be . . . that no harsh measures would be taken against him.' Aba's fingers were sliding across the newspaper, blurring the print.

'Yes,' Hasan said. 'Ami told me. Because the foreign powers wouldn't let the President harm him.'

'Right. But it seems that the President's been in touch

with . . . well, a whole bunch of foreign powers, and he's signed trade agreements with each of them. So he's going to export just about anything he can, just about anything we produce and the rest of the world needs. And usually export is a pretty good thing, because we get something in return.'

'Aba, you don't have to explain that.'

'Sorry. But, in the case of this particular trade agreement we're getting a really minimal amount in return for our exports. At least, officially. In monetary terms.'

'So what are we getting unofficially?'

'Well, not us. Just the President. He's getting *carte blanche*.' Aba closed his eyes and leaned back, shaking his head.

'What's that?'

Hasan knew how disturbed Aba must be when he didn't answer and it was up to Ami to say, 'Permission to do what he likes.'

'Oh,' Hasan said. 'So . . .' he tried not to sound too worried. 'So what's the sentence for treason? How many years?'

Aba looked up, a few inches above Hasan's head. Hasan felt Ami's chin move left-right-left against his hair. 'Well, there are variables,' Aba said. 'It is a serious offence, but there are variables.' He looked back down at the newspaper and began to speak rapidly. 'You'd think they would at least mention Salman somewhere. Although, I suppose they're making a mockery of censorship, carrying it to an extreme, preferring omission to saying the kind of nonsense the government feeds them. I can't blame them for being scared.'

'Perhaps they're not as scared as you think,' Ami said, leaning forward and running her finger down a column of newsprint. 'Read vertically. Read only the first letter of each line in each article's lead column.'

Hasan followed the path of her fingertip. 'P-I-N-E C-O-N-E-S,' he read out loud. 'PINE CONES PINE CONES PINE CONES PINE CONES PINE PINE PINE PINE PINE PINE PINE SALMAN.'

Hasan's heart surged at the sight of Salman Mamoo's name in print for the first time in three months. He pictured Salman Mamoo's supporters stitching together a hundred copies of the front page and floating it magic-carpet-style through Salman Mamoo's cell window at 6.00 p.m. in place of pine-cones.

'What is this meant to accomplish?' Aba said. 'What are they thinking?'

Hasan leapt out of his chair. It had come upon him again, that old feeling of a spring curling and uncurling in his stomach as it did when he was five and Salman Mamoo pushed the garden swing higher and faster. Hasan ran round the garden, ran past hibiscus, bougainvillaea and kumquat trees, leapt up, swung on the branch of a guava tree, back and forth and back and forth and back and his leg kicked the invisible goblin. Aha! Got you! He threw himself on the ground before the goblin could recover from the blow, rolled over and over until he reached the cricket bat which became an oak staff the moment his hand touched it. He threw it high, caught it on the descent, shifted it from hand to hand to hand so fast it became a blur of possibility . . . and the goblin, always a coward, ran away. Hasan kissed the bat and saw the Widow, just feet away, watching him.

'I want to know,' Hasan said, in his most adult voice. 'What's the penalty for treason?'

For the first time ever, Hasan saw the Widow look taken aback. She turned slightly to glance at her bedroom window, and for a moment Hasan thought she would leave. But, instead, her hand went to her throat. It was all the response Hasan needed.

'Oh, my dear,' she said, coming towards him. 'If only I could show you the way into my world.'

Then Uncle Latif was there, holding Hasan, down on his knees, and Hasan was surprised to find that he was kneeling too. 'Let it out, Huss. Let it out,' Uncle Latif said. But Hasan kept his eyes wide and dry. Salamander, he told himself. Salamander, first meaning. He broke out of Uncle Latif's grasp and went charging around the garden, feet pounding and hands fisted, giving his heart a good reason to pump so madly.

Chapter Eleven

Hasan dragged his throbbing legs into his room. Ami's voice called to him but he yelled back, 'Can't come now. Nature calls!' and shut the door behind him. He leaned against the door and allowed his body to slide to the ground, his hair squeaking and bristling in its descent along the white-washed wood. Now what? he wondered, hugging his knees to his chest. He looked around. Something was different. His bed. The blue summer coverlet had made its appearance.

Hasan crawled across the room, pulled himself on the bed and ran his hands in circles along his coverlet in greeting. Ami must have removed his duvet last night or this morning. The thought was cheering. If Salman Mamoo's situation really were desperate Ami would not have concerned herself with bedspreads.

It seemed that for once, though, Ami had entered his room without rearranging his bookshelf. Hasan ran a proprietary eye along the books across the room from him. Both Ami and Zehra had reacted strongly when Hasan arranged his books alphabetically. 'It looks so ragged,' Ami had complained. And Zehra had just rolled her eyes and said, 'First, books are alphabetized by author, not title. Second, it's not like you've got an entire rainforest worth of books. Tall to short, favourite to least favourite. Those are the only acceptable categories. No need to get democratic about books, okay?' This was the day after the military coup, and seemed unfair. So Hasan did not tell Zehra about the comfort of order, or the reassurance of knowing that every new book would have a place already awaiting it, or the thrill of finding alliterations by stringing together the first words (articles aside) of titles: Hagar Hamlet Haroun Harry Higher Hookey Hockey Horse.

Hasan closed his eyes. A is for ACE, he thought. A is for the day Salman Mamoo first mentioned the name Anti-Corruption Enterprise, the day after he resigned his portfolio and addressed the crowds who met him at the City's airport, his voice lowering just when everyone expected it to rise, lowering to an intimacy as he said, 'Give your imaginations a little freedom again. There are few realities that can withstand collective belief. Let me tell you something I've often imagined of late . . . a political party called the Anti-Corruption Enterprise.'

B is for Beach. Salman Mamoo's favourite haunt, the one place that beat anything the North had to offer. It was Salman Mamoo who taught Hasan how to hypnotize himself by rocking back and forth on his heels on the wet sand, watching his toe imprints fill with water and disappear. And it was Salman Mamoo also who agreed it would be a travesty to squeeze into shoes for the car ride home just when one's toes had spread so wide apart they could cover the length of a two-week old turtle's shell.

C is for Cricket . . .

Hasan had made his way through the English alphabet and had progressed to *zal* in Urdu when a foot kicked open his door, and Zehra walked in bearing a plate of chicken tikkas in one hand, and a plate of *na'an* in the other. Ogle bounded in after her, and darted forward to grab Hasan's socks in his mouth. As these were still on Hasan's feet there was a momentary scuffle, from which both emerged triumphant. Ogle, with one sock dangling from his mouth; Hasan with one sock on his right foot. Zehra, sitting cross-legged at the foot of the bed, rolled her eyes. 'Og! Drop!' she commanded. The Labrador spat out the sock and lunged for Hasan's right foot. Hasan jumped backwards and hit his head against the wall.

'Ow!' he growled, glaring at Ogle.

The dog retreated to a corner, and contented himself with chewing on a slipper.

'I don't know what's got into him today,' Zehra said. 'He's never this frisky in the afternoon.'

'Remember why you named him?'

'Hmm . . . his connection to the Prez.'

'Yeah,' Hasan said, taking a lemon-slice between his fingers and squeezing it with a vigour that far exceeded the lemon's capacity to provide juice. 'Well, I bet he's frisky today.'

Zehra didn't say anything, but handed Hasan the hottest *na'an*, the one at the bottom of the stack. Hasan smiled. He had made the same gesture of consolation and sympathy towards Zehra when her mother died, years ago. Or so Zehra had once told him. For her that moment marked the beginning of their friendship, though Hasan couldn't remember the gesture any more than he could remember a time when he and Zehra weren't friends. Hasan shook his head. Zehra's mother's death had nothing to do with Salman Mamoo's situation. Nothing.

Hasan bounced the *na'an* from palm to palm, not allowing it to settle in one spot long enough to burn him. When it had cooled just a fraction, he ripped off a piece and bit into it, savouring, with closed eyes, its mixture of lightness, chewiness, and warmth.

'You know, all the clichés about love are also true for food,' Zehra observed, her pinched fingers holding a piece of *na'an* over the fleshiest part of the chicken breast. With a flick of her wrist she tore a piece of meat off the bone, and popped *na'an* and chicken into her mouth. Food is blind? Hasan considered this for a moment and decided – yes, true enough. All conversation stopped while Hasan and Zehra chewed on the chicken's mix of charred exterior and succulent interior, bound together by Imran's 'mystical spices'. When they had devoured the meat, the room filled with the sound of paper-thin ribs cracking between Hasan's teeth, interspersed with the ring of tongue-smacking as Zehra sucked the spices off her fingers.

'So, what have you heard?' Hasan asked.

Zehra squeezed lemon juice on her fingers to cut the grease and shrugged. 'Not a lot. Just that Uncle Salman's trial is on the nineteenth of next month. You didn't know that?'

Hasan shook his head. 'I guess that's what Ami wanted to tell me,' he said. 'Good. So he should be free before the summer holidays start.' He avoided Zehra's eye. There was silence again.

'Why doesn't Uncle Shehryar disconnect the phone?' Zehra asked finally. 'It keeps ringing every five minutes.'

'I don't know. I guess in case someone calls with news about how to help Salman Mamoo. I mean, Aba must know someone who can help.'

Zehra toyed with her wishbone for a few seconds before

blurting out, 'Look, grown-ups can't always fix things. I know. I mean, I didn't always know and so I was angry with my father. And even now, sometimes, I want to yell at him because if it had been her liver or her kidneys that would have been one thing, but it just seems he should have known if something was wrong with her heart.'

'It's not the same thing,' Hasan said. 'Look, I should go and sit with my parents. I'll come over later.'

Hasan followed Zehra and Ogle out of the room, then turned towards his parents' room with some reluctance. The phone rang the moment he entered the room. 'My turn,' Ami said. 'Hello . . . oh, Farah Apa . . . No, just that the trial is next month. On the nineteenth.'

Hasan turned to Aba. 'So, any calls about Salman Mamoo?'

Aba managed his lop-sided smile. 'About fifty! But all just questions. Oh, except for one a few minutes ago. I answered, and this man on the other end identified himself as a party worker. I said, "I'm really not in a festive mood. Try calling the President," and, of course, it turned out he meant . . .'

'Political party.'

'Hmmm. You probably should have answered the phone.'

'Oh, Aba! Was he offended?'

'I believe so. He said, "I mean POTPAF." I said, "POTPAF yourself." So he said, "Party Of The Present And Future. That is the Anti-Corruption Enterprise's new name."'

'ACE has become POTPAF!'

'I presume this was done without Salman's approval. Anyway, once we had established that the caller wasn't a waiter or a bartender he said he was calling all Salman's supporters who weren't DICOOC . . .'

'What?'

'Dead, In Coma, or Out Of Country. So, the party . . .'

'POTPAF!' Hasan laughed louder than he would have at any other time. At least Aba was trying to be normal.

'Yes. POTPAF is arranging a protest rally this evening.'

Hasan stopped laughing instantly. 'Where?'

'We're not going.'

'Why not?'

'Listen, Huss. These are dangerous days. Now more so than before. So for all our sakes you mustn't talk to anyone about Salman or the President. Understood?'

'I know that already, Aba. I never say anything, except to Zehra. But why can't we go?'

'I have a feeling this rally will be an opportunity for people in the party to stir up trouble, and we'll only get hurt if we're a part of it. God knows I admire the struggle, but there are certain prices I cannot pay to assist it.' Hasan's mouth tightened, and Aba added, 'I would rather live under a dictator and have Salman safe at home, than achieve democracy through his imprisonment.' Hasan had been looking above Aba's head at Ami's newest painting, watching for the moment when the strokes of greens and browns would transform themselves into suggestions of shapes, but now he snapped his attention back to Aba's face; had it been his imagination or had Aba paused, almost fumbled, before the word 'imprisonment'?

Aba held up his hand. 'I know. You think it's cowardice, and it's true that I'm placing my needs above the greater good, but if it is cowardice it's based not on fear, but on love. Is any of this getting through to you?'

'Yes,' Hasan said shortly. 'You wish Salman Mamoo would agree to give up politics and make a statement supporting military rule.'

'Well, I don't know about that. He would hate himself, you know. Besides, it's people like your Salman Mamoo who change the world. And son, it needs changing.'

Hasan turned his attention to the newspaper's comic strips. Aba had always laughed at people who offered up morals and capsule philosophies; he said it revealed the quantity of bad television that people watched. 'Roll credits,' Hasan muttered, making sure Aba couldn't decipher his words.

Ami ended her phone conversation and turned to Aba. 'That was Farah Apa. She wants to come over so of course I told her not to think of leaving her house with the situation as volatile as it is. But she'll be over this way later, for her nephew's – little Azeem's – *chehlum*.'

Forty days! Forty days since a yellow kite had offered Azeem flight, and his body had realized, too late, its limitations. Forty days, and tonight the period of mourning would be over.

'. . . so I told her we would go with her.'

'But, Saira, we barely know the boy's parents.'

'Yes, I know. But they're practically our neighbours now and with all the riots there aren't likely to be many people there. I'm sure they would appreciate it if we went. Besides I can't just go on sitting by the phone all day.'

'Well, you and Hasan go. I'll sit by the phone. But right now I'm going to eat some of that chicken Latif sent over. Want some?'

Ami shook her head. When Aba had gone she turned to Hasan and said, 'What is it about Azeem that brings that look to your face?'

'I told you. I saw him on his roof while he was flying his kite.'

'Are you sure that's all you saw?'

'I told you, Ami. I saw him fly his kite and then I went inside. It's weird, that's all, to know that just a few minutes later he . . . you know.'

Ami was looking at him with an expression she had last displayed when he had claimed a splitting headache just minutes before Zehra came to pick him up for Najam's birthday party. Fortunately the phone rang again and Hasan left the room the moment Ami picked up the receiver.

He found himself in Ami's studio, looking at the calendar on the wall. He flipped to the previous month and counted one day at a time. Yes, it really had been forty days. He turned to the next page and placed his finger on the nineteenth. He snaked the finger backwards. One week, two weeks – page flip – three weeks, four weeks and one, two, three, four days plus today. The finger stopped. Another forty days until Salman Mamoo's trial. Hasan rested his head against the calendar and wondered if life henceforth would be a journey from grief to grief.

A mug of soapy water stood on a stool beside Hasan. He picked up a piece of wire, bent its end into a circle, dipped it into the water and blew out a stream of bubbles. Each bubble led into another, one ending so that another could begin, each a swirl of colours, brightest before it burst into nothing and left Hasan staring through a wire loop.

Chapter Twelve

Ami and Aba took it so much for granted that Hasan would go to the *chehlum* that he did not bother to argue. Just as well to let someone else make that decision for him; he felt personally incapable of deciding if he would rather stay at home or not. He showered, ironed his *shalwar kameez*, put a piece of scotch tape over the rip in his *shalwar*, and was ready, on-the-dot punctual, when Farah Khala's car drew up to the gate. Hasan was curious about how he would react to the *chehlum* but he surprised himself by feeling nothing, except thirst, when he walked through Azeem's gate. Ami and Farah Khala disappeared into the house with the other women mourners, and Farah Khala's son, Ali Bhai, cousin to both Hasan and Azeem, guided Hasan further into the garden.

'That's Azeem's father,' Ali Bhai said, bending down, nearly doubled over, to speak into Hasan's ear. He pointed in the direction of the bougainvillaea where a group of men stood shaking their heads and smiling the way people do when they are about to cry.

'Which one?' Hasan asked.

'The one with the beard. Come on, I'll introduce you,' Ali Bhai said, taking Hasan's hand.

Hasan shook his head. 'Too many people. You go. Introduce me later.' Ali Bhai nodded, patted Hasan on the back and disappeared into the crowd. He's put on weight since his wedding, Hasan thought. It was at Ali Bhai's wedding that Hasan had met Azeem and, amidst the fairy-lights and flash-photography and swirls of silk, Azeem from the North, boy of hill-stations who sometimes awoke to find clouds creeping into his bedroom through the cracked open window, had confirmed what Hasan had always suspected. 'Of course people can fly,' he said. 'My elder cousin says she has, but she also says it's something you must do in the secrecy of night.' Was that it? Hasan wondered. Did daylight kill Azeem?

Something shiny glinted in the bushes near the verandah. Hasan squatted on the grass and pulled the thing into view. It was a roller-skate. Hasan turned it around in his hands: yes, this was the same make of skate as the ones Ali Bhai had given Hasan for his birthday last year. The day he had ripped apart red shiny paper to reveal the skates Hasan had even tried sleeping with them on his feet, but that turned out to be a practice most enticing in the abstract. Still, his grief had been quite profound when a wheel snapped off the left skate. Hasan examined the skate in his hand more closely, spinning the wheels one by one and running them over his palm. This, too, was a left-footed skate. He put it down on the ground and lined it up with his foot. Same size.

'Oh,' he said out loud, only just realizing what he was doing. He picked up the skate with both hands and set it down amongst the bushes before walking quickly away.

Halfway across the verandah he looked back. It's not as though anyone else is going to use it now, he reasoned. Enough, he told himself. Enough!

Hasan looked around. Glass sliding doors separated him from the drawing room where Ami sat cross-legged with the other women on a large white sheet. While Hasan watched she rocked forward, scooped up a fistful of kidney-beans from the pile running along the centre of the sheet, rocked back and let each bean fall from her fingers with a prayer. He could see her body relaxing in a trance of ritual, her lips moving in a steady rhythm, her thumb flicking each kidney-bean from her palm to her thumb and forefinger where it rotated for the duration of a whispered prayer before falling, falling . . .

Hasan started and turned his eyes away. His gaze landed on the bright yellow flowers of the laburnum tree. He tilted his head back to look at the roof. This was the spot. Hasan stepped forward into the shade of the laburnum. He closed his eyes and saw Azeem frozen in descent, just to the right of the laburnum. He opened his eyes and the image of the falling boy shimmered before him, translucent and shot-through with rainbows. Hasan outstretched his arms. One step forwards and he would have him.

'Hasan?'

Hasan swung around. A man with the passing familiarity of a third cousin was looking at him.

'Hasan, right? Saira's son?'

Hasan nodded.

'You don't remember me. I'm your cousin Ali's brother-in-law, Taimur.' Hasan feigned recognition. The man went on. 'I just wanted to say I'm praying for your Uncle Salman. Everyone is.'

'You're Salman Haq's nephew?' a second man said. 'No joke! Really?'

Hasan turned around. Azeem's image was gone. Everywhere he heard 'Salman . . . Salman'; men waiting around for the sound of the *azaan* so that they could pray for Azeem were gathering around him asking, 'Any news from your uncle? Is it true your family's planning to leave the country? When did you hear?' and then one squeaky voice: 'Who's going to represent Salman at the trial?'

The *azaan* cut through all talk. The men ambled towards the far end of the garden where, between wooden poles holding up a paisleyed canopy, four overlapping white sheets weighed down by stones served as a giant prayer-mat. But Hasan stayed where he was, one hand clapped to the top of his skull. Of course, he thought. Of course! Aba will represent Salman Mamoo and there's no way he won't win. After all, Aba's the best lawyer in the City and Salman Mamoo's innocent to boot.

To boot, to boot, to boot, Hasan sang to himself, skipping towards the prayer area. Halfway there he remembered propriety and slowed to a shuffle. The cluster of men bustling across the white sheets resolved itself into rows and columns, and a cloth-capped man detached himself from the main body and prepared to lead the prayers. Hasan weighed the impropriety of running at a funeral against the impropriety of arriving late for prayer, and sprinted the last few steps to an empty spot beside Ali Bhai.

As one the assembled men placed hands parallel to heads, thumbs touching shoulders, placed hands one on top of the other against chests, bent, knelt, prostrated themselves, lips moving in Arabic. One by one, then in twos and threes they closed their eyes. Hasan recalled the calm of alphabetizing books.

While he was kneeling he felt a touch against his cheeks. He opened his eyes and something winged glided past. Dusk-fairy. Hasan was about to lower his lids when he became aware of Ali Bhai winking at him. That certainly seemed inappropriate. Hasan, lips still moving, turned his head and saw that Ali Bhai was actually pretending his eyes were closed while really keeping one eye slightly open and fixed on Azeem's father who was kneeling in front of him.

Hasan had to stifle a laugh. A brief flirtation with atheism had cost Ali Bhai the ability to recall the rituals to prayer, and no matter how often his younger cousins reminded him when to stand, when to kneel, when to bow, he always misplaced the information just when he needed to put it to use.

Azeem's father bent forward and touched his forehead to the sheet. In his haste not to be left behind Ali Bhai jerked his torso downward with greater velocity than necessary and his forehead bounced off the ground. He stifled a moan. Hasan sucked in his cheeks and bit down on them before he recalled he was not merely an observer in this scene and closed the distance between his head and the sheet.

This forehead-to-the-ground posture posed immediate problems for Hasan's enjoyment of Ali Bhai's predicament. His eyes could not see anything but white sheet with occasional blades of grass poking through. But no doubt Ali Bhai faced the same dilemma. Hasan turned his head sideways so that his left eye could see Ali Bhai and, at that moment, Ali Bhai turned his head sideways and his right eye looked straight at Hasan. There was a movement of bodies all around. Ali Bhai sprang to his feet, and Hasan followed suit without thinking. Everyone else was kneeling. Ali Bhai and Hasan crashed down on their knees. Now a number of eyes were open and distracted from God. The ultimate

97

upstage, Hasan thought, and hoped his shoulders weren't shaking as much as were Ali Bhai's. Through all the confusion Hasan had continued reciting prayers in his head. He couldn't quite decide if that was extreme piety or ultimate irreverence.

The prayer reached its conclusion and the men cupped their hands inches away from their faces to offer up individual blessings for Azeem's soul. Hasan held his hands right against his face in an attempt to smooth his mouth into a straight line. He peeked between thumb and forefinger at Ali Bhai. Ali Bhai's face was very still and his eyes were closed like traps. From the house next door came the sound of laughter. Without warning, Hasan felt himself flush with rage. He wanted to leap over the wall and physically knock down whoever was laughing. Wanted to cry out, 'He's dead, he's dead. How dare you laugh today!' Hasan bowed his head. 'Please,' he whispered, his voice splintering in the hollow of his palm. 'Please, oh please. Please. I'll do anything, just . . . please.' His body rocked back and forth and back and forth until the whole world was rocking and he no longer knew what he was saying or why or to whom or how to stop or what else he could ever do in his life but this. 'Please, please.'

'Hasan.' Ami drew his hands away from his face and held them tightly in her own. Hasan blinked and looked around. He was the only one left under the canopy. The garden lights had been switched on, and brass dishes piled high with steaming *biryani* formed a dissecting line along the length of yet another white sheet. Azeem's father stood up from his cross-legged position at the edge of the sheet and walked towards Hasan with a plate of *biryani* in his hand.

'Eat,' he said. 'Sometimes what we think is grief turns out to be hunger. That's why the famine-stricken always look so unhappy.'

Hasan wasn't quite sure how to respond to this so he merely took the plate, trying to look sombre and grateful and edified in the same moment. Ami led him indoors to eat with the women. 'Aren't I too old to be allowed in here,' Hasan said, slipping off his shoes outside the drawing room and scanning the room for two empty spots where he and Ami could squeeze in as unobtrusively as possible.

Ami smiled, and pretended not to. 'Of course you are. But nobody will mind.'

More white sheets lay wall to wall in the room. Hasan wondered if the sheets had been bought for the occasion, or just borrowed. Perhaps Azeem's family had a thing for white sheets. Hasan had only once been to a *chehlum* before, but he couldn't recall who had died, let alone the quantity and colours of sheets laid down. Hasan picked at his plate and swallowed grains of rice, one by one. Of course, there had been Nana's *chehlum* as well, but all Hasan could recall of the events surrounding his grandfather's death was Ami putting an arm around Salman Mamoo's neck and saying, 'So, we're orphans now.' Oh, and undoubtedly there had been a *chehlum* for Zehra's mother. Hasan picked apart a piece of chicken into thin strips. All these deaths, he thought. For a moment he looked at the piece of chicken and considered vegetarianism, but his stomach sent urgent override messages to his brain, and Hasan bowed his head in gratitude and shovelled *biryani* into his mouth.

'They say the quality of food at a *chehlum* reflects the quality of the deceased person's life,' said a corpulent woman near Hasan. 'And I have to say, though I'm full I can't stop eating.'

'Azeem was too pure for this world,' another woman said.

'So delightful, God could not be apart from him any longer.'

When Farah Khala dropped Ami and Hasan home, Hasan asked, 'Is Salman Mamoo pure?'

Ami bit her lip. 'No, he isn't.'

'Promise?'

'Promise.'

Chapter Thirteen

'No. Salman's going to be tried in a military court. No civilians allowed, not even civilian lawyers.' Aba held the ice-tray under the hot-water tap and twisted his wrists this way and that until there was a crackle of dislodging ice. Visitors had been dropping in all evening and all night, and Atif-Asif-Arif's fingers had turned to prunes with the endless washing of tea-cups. There had been three cars parked outside the house when Ami and Hasan returned from the *chehlum* and by nine-thirty the row of cars had extended all the way down to the pink house, prompting passers-by to tell the Bodyguard that it was absolutely disgraceful the way the élite behave . . . throwing a party on a day of national calamity.

Gul Mumani and Ami shook their heads at each visitor saying, 'You shouldn't have left the house. Things are so dangerous,' but everyone claimed to know a safe route home. Still, Hasan noticed that cars arrived and left in tandem, and none of the visitors lived beyond a five-mile radius from Hasan's house. At first Hasan had wanted the visitors to leave;

their gloomy expressions, hugs of commiseration and incessant patting of Gul Mumani's hands seemed a particularly perverse form of torture. But then Auntie Chinnoo got the hiccups, prompting everyone to proffer tried-and-tested remedies, and oh! the horror on Uncle Aslam's face when he entered the room and saw his wife kick off her shoes, rise up on her toes, hold her breath and circle her arms, clockwise, through the air. With that, everything changed. Aba and Uncle Javed threw themselves into a rematch of their college thumb-wrestling contest; Auntie Naz attempted to perform card trick upon card trick, each more hilariously unsuccessful than the last, until Ami picked a card and Auntie Naz grabbed it out of her hand, glanced at it, shoved it back in the deck and said, 'There! It's the six of clubs.' Ami, nearly incoherent with laughter, said, 'Nine of clubs, actually'; Gul Mumani remembered her teenaged efforts to impress the French boy who sat beside her in class by passing him a note consisting of the only French she knew: *voulez vous*. Spelling was never Gul Mumani's strong suit, and the boy looked down at 'Woo Lay Woo' and sent back the scrawled message: 'Chinese porno film?'; and, just when the glum-faced arrival of Uncle Poppy and Auntie Poops threatened to destroy all levity in the room, Uncle Latif donned white pyjamas, black shirt and white jacket, and swivelled his hips into the TV room, singing 'Night Fever' in falsetto.

And through it all Hasan had hugged his knees to his chest and laughed louder than anyone else, thinking 'Aba's going to save Salman Mamoo'. But now, with a single utterance – 'No' – Aba had ruined everything.

'What good are you?' Hasan burst out. The words quivered in the air for the briefest of moments, and Hasan wanted to reach out and stuff them back in his mouth even if they

102

choked him. Even as he thought that, he knew he couldn't say it out loud because some part of him wanted Aba to believe he meant the accusation.

Aba pressed the tips of his fingers against the top of an ice-cube and watched the cube turn into water with the pressure. 'Not much good,' he said. 'You know, I've always maintained that ninety per cent of all action should take place here –' he tapped what remained of the ice-cube against his skull. 'And if I work hard enough at the ninety per cent I can make the remaining ten per cent palatable . . . I mean, the mind, Hasan, the mind. Its sheer capacity!' Hasan looked back blankly, but Aba was in what Ami called 'the Throes'. Hasan could see the last of the visitors leave, but Aba made no attempt to go and see them off though he could not have missed the high-pitched goodbyes of Auntie Shehla. Perhaps Aba noticed Hasan's incomprehension, because he made backflipping motions with his hands. 'Let me put this differently,' Aba said.

He leaned against the counter, seemingly oblivious to the cubes of ice melting and soaking his sleeve. 'For Salman, time is pendular.' He pulled a piece of string out of the kitchen drawer, shook some salt on to a piece of ice, and held one end of the string against the salty surface of the ice. For a couple of seconds he just stood there, holding up a finger for silence and then he raised the hand holding the string. The ice rose off the counter, attached to the salted string. Hasan's eyes opened wide. Aba flicked a finger against the ice. String and ice started swaying back and forth. 'For Salman, time is pendular,' Aba repeated, pointing to the ice. 'That's why he's such a nostalgist, always talking about his uncle's glorious governance. See, to Salman, nostalgia is hope; to me, it's usually loss. Linear time, that's my view.' Aba flicked the ice again with more power, and the ice flew across the room to smash against the fridge, leaving Aba holding a dangling string.

Hasan felt as though he had heard this – or something like it – before, but he couldn't see what it had to do with Aba's inability to represent Salman Mamoo. 'Okay, I'm building up to something resembling a point,' Aba said, absent-mindedly rolling up his sleeve and chucking the remaining blobs of ice into the ice-bucket. 'Given Salman's situation, my belief in linear time gives me hope.' The Throes again. 'Situations don't necessarily have to keep recurring. It's just that people generally have such limited imaginations that originality seldom occurs. But that doesn't have to be the case. So what if there are no historical precedents for a completely happy ending? So what if the happiest ending that comes to mind is one which requires erstwhile good-guys to use the tools of a tyrant? So what? We can play with ideas until we think of a new precedent and then . . . apply it.'

'Aba,' Hasan sighed. 'I'm eleven years old.'

'A valid observation. Basically I'm saying, don't give up.'

Hasan thumbs-upped his approval of this sentiment. Yet another visitor walked up to the front door. Aba peered out and his eyebrows shot up. 'Huss, can you sit out of this visit.' It wasn't a question. 'I'll explain later,' Aba said and almost ran out of the kitchen. Hasan tried to decipher the expression that had lit up Aba's face, and decided it was hope. Something linear must have happened, he told himself.

He retrieved Yorker from his bedroom and wandered outside to sit with the Bodyguard, seven in number this evening. Zehra was on her knees just outside the Bodyguard's circle, braiding the greying hair of Razia Bibi, smoker of imported cigarettes.

'No school tomorrow, I suppose,' Hasan said to Zehra.

Zehra frowned at him. 'Don't be rude. Speak Urdu. Although –' she glanced around, grinning, and switched to English herself, 'I bet they all understand English, right?'

Khalida-the-Heartbreaker laughed. 'No school. More strike,' she said in English.

There were whistles and applause all around, but the loudest and deepest roar of approval was missing. 'Where's Khan?' Hasan asked. Khan was the one constant in the ever-shifting composition of the Bodyguard. He was also the only member of the Bodyguard to whom the Widow ever spoke, though he only acquired that distinction last year when Uncle Latif hired him to replace the family's narcoleptic driver. 'Where is he?' Hasan said, surprising himself with the brittleness of his voice.

It transpired Khan's brother-in-law was missing. He had not returned home to Khan's sister the night before and this morning rumour arrived that two plain-clothes policemen had picked him up just near the tea-stand at which he often stopped on his way home from work. Khan had gone to make inquiries at the central police station.

'It is a stupid thing to do,' said Khalida. 'With all the riots and killing, and now curfew clamped in thirteen different districts, I don't know how he even expects to reach the police station.'

Mansoor-with-the-long-thumbnail saw an opportunity to discredit his chief rival for Khalida's affection, and hastened to jump into the conversation. 'Well, he's either hiding down the road, hoping you're impressed with his bravery in the face of death, or he's emptied his brain of common sense and, since no buses are running today, is walking ten miles to the police station. Whatever the case, he's either a liar or a fool.'

Razia Bibi clucked her tongue in disdain. 'Khan's no liar,

105

and as for being a fool . . . if a man isn't a fool where his family is concerned, I have no respect for him.'

There were murmurs of agreement, and Khalida said, 'Well, we will all pray for his return. Even if it means staying awake all night in supplication. Will you join us, Hasan?'

'Ask the Widow that,' Hasan laughed. 'Can you imagine anyone asking her to skip her sleep for one night. Even in order to pray.'

'Oh, she doesn't need to pray,' said a voice behind Hasan. 'Why, every moment of all our lives is a prayer for her well-being in this life and the next, so even if she were to give in to debauchery for the rest of her life, when she dies our combined prayers will wrap around her like a shroud and carry her along the path to heaven which only prayers know of.'

'From philosopher to poet,' Khalida smiled up at Khan, causing Mansoor to scowl. 'What news of your brother?'

Khan sat down, angling his body carefully as though his back were made of cardboard that would crease if bent. 'Nothing good. For most of the day my shoes just collected dust, going this way and that, taking roundabout routes to avoid the curfew areas. The streets were more silent than sleep – shells of torched buses everywhere. At last I came near the central station, but it was surrounded by curfew areas. So I stood outside the curfew zone, counting the hairs in my beard until the curfew lifted for an hour.' He stopped and ran a finger along a crack in his sole. Mansoor rolled his eyes at the drama of the telling, but even he edged closer when Khan started again in a whisper.

But now Hasan was no longer listening to Khan because he was walking with Khan through the curfew zone, watching men – ACEmen, some barely older than Hasan – form human shields around the groups of women who strode, stone-eyed,

106

to the market to buy up all the provisions in stock from shop-keepers who – by and large, by and large – made no fuss about buying on credit. Uniformed men crouched behind sandbags with fingers on triggers and did not so much as turn their heads when two tanks rolled up. Khan kept his head down and looked innocuous enough to pass unmolested through the makeshift checkpoints which had sprung up at every turning with an efficiency that was chillingly unfamiliar to the City.

But at the police station the gates were locked, though men and women with sweat stains shaped like continents on their clothes stuck hands and faces through the grilles of the gate and cried, 'My son . . . my husband . . .' And one anguished cry, 'Oh God, my daughter.' Khan saw it was useless and started to walk away when a young man – well-dressed, booted and suited – touched Khan's arm and said, 'I know where you can get news of your brother-in-law.'

'But Khan, how did he know who you were looking for?' Zehra asked.

'Zehra, when you haven't eaten meat for a week and some-one offers you a bowl of *piya* you don't stop to ask him where he got the goats for it,' Khan said. 'Even if you know it'll give you indigestion.'

'So then?' Mansoor demanded.

'Well, he said to go to the newspaper office. Told me there were lists there of people killed resisting arrest or attempting to defy state authority. So I started walking again, but Akhtar saw me with my broken sole and said his bike would get him to the newspaper office and back here in quick-time. He should be here soon.'

'But what would the police want with your brother-in-law?' Hasan said.

Khan rubbed blades of grass together and made the patch of lawn sing squeaky laments. 'He's an ardent supporter of your uncle.'

'So are most people I know,' Hasan said.

'Yes,' Khan acknowledged. 'In their hearts and in their drawing rooms. Besides, wealth changes things.' Hasan looked down, and fingered the cuff of his jeans.

'Here comes Akhtar,' Razia Bibi said.

Akhtar sprung off his bike and rushed to Khan with a list, not even pausing to pull down the wheel-rest. The bike crashed down on Uncle Latif's sloping driveway, wheels spinning frantically. Khan took the list and handed it to Zehra. 'It's in English,' he said.

Zehra slid a finger down the page, her lips moving silently. A few inches from the bottom of the column of print, her finger stopped.

'I'm sorry, Khan,' she said.

'Where is it? Which is his name?'

Zehra's finger underlined the words 'Gohar, son of Asghar'. Hasan was amazed she knew which name to look for. Khan prised open the blade on his pocket-knife and cut out his brother-in-law's name from the page. 'I'll give this to my sister,' he said. 'At least it's something.' He traced the letters, right to left. 'He could read English, you know.'

'Oh,' said Hasan. His cheeks were burning, and he felt as though he should feel guilty about something. 'I have to go,' he mumbled, standing up. He wanted to hug Khan, but that would mean walking halfway around the circle and drawing attention to himself.

Once inside, Hasan made his way into his bedroom. He had just shut the door behind him when the door to the TV room opened. A foreign-accented female voice emerged.

'Believe me, I'm sorry about this. For the record, though of course, off the record, I admire Salman –' she pronounced it as if it were 'sall-mun' – 'and even consider him a friend. But my hands are tied. Coming to see you is as far as I can go in contravening my government's directives.'

'Your government made a great show of support for Salman, not so long ago,' Ami cut in.

'Saira, what can I say? That trade agreement . . .'

'Is bribery!' said Ami.

'Perhaps, but my country is getting real benefits from it. You can't expect us to place your well-being over our well-being. And it's not just the trade agreement. There are other strategic reasons why we can't alienate your President.'

'You've been rehearsing that all day, haven't you?' Aba said drily.

'All week, actually,' the woman said.

'All week! You mean to tell me . . .'

'One other thing,' the woman went on, as though Aba's interruption had not occurred.

'Yes?'

'I know I'm not the only person of influence you have tried to contact. Give it up. The risk is too great and there will be no dividends.'

Three sets of footsteps echoed down the hall. Hasan poked his head out of his room, but could find nothing familiar about the back of the woman who was walking out of the front door with Ami and Aba. Hasan walked over to the TV room and froze in the doorway. Gul Mumani was in the room, staring up at a painting of Salman Mamoo and Aba, dressed in their cricketing whites. Salman Mamoo's collar button was undone and his head was thrown back in laughter. Gul Mumani placed the tip of her index finger against Salman

Mamoo's hint of an Adam's apple. The finger began to move side to side along Salman Mamoo's throat; a gentle caress, now pressing down harder, faster, a thing beyond Gul Mumani's control, whipping from left to right to left until it was a frenzy Hasan could no longer bear to watch. He walked away before Gul Mumani knew he was there, but he was never again able to brush skin against canvas without a shudder rippling down his spine.

Chapter Fourteen

At first Hasan thought it had merely been hunger. French toast and sweet, milky tea dispelled all stomach somersaults so completely Hasan began to think the fear he had woken up with was merely a hunger so intense it defied immediate categorization. But when Ami entered the kitchen, red cracks at the corners of her eyes gravitating towards her pupils, Hasan's stomach turned gymnastic again.

'Any news about Salman Mamoo?' he asked, pushing away his plate.

Ami moved aside a jar of tea-leaves and reached for the coffee at the back of the cabinet. 'No. Nothing. The Bodyguard reports nearly a hundred people were killed in the riots yesterday, in the City alone. I have a feeling you're not going back to school for a while.'

'Is Aba going to the office?'

'Not today. ACE has extended the strike indefinitely.'

'POTPAF,' Hasan corrected her, but it didn't seem to lighten her mood. She stirred boiling water into her coffee and came to stand beside Hasan.

'You hate coffee,' he reminded her.

Ami wrinkled her nose in agreement and pushed the mug away. 'Gul's moving in. Your father's taken her to pick up her things.'

Hasan had thought he was the first one awake. 'I wonder what prison's like,' he said.

Ami covered Hasan's eyes with her hands. 'A blank canvas,' she said. 'See it?' Hasan nodded. Five blank canvases, joined together to form the five sides of a cube. Floor, ceiling and three walls. The canvases grew four, six, eight feet tall as he watched them, and became the grey of dirt and sweat and thoughts staled by repetition. Slashes of light rent through the far wall of canvas and shaded the grey to end its monotony. Salman Mamoo appeared in a shaft of light, arms akimbo, and surveyed the canvases. He did not see Hasan standing behind him in the place where a sixth canvas was needed to complete the cube. Hasan didn't mind.

Salman Mamoo walked over to a wall-canvas, produced some glinting object from his pocket and began to scratch the grey paint. He's trying to scratch through the canvas, Hasan thought. That'll take for ever. But no, Salman Mamoo was etching calligraphy on the wall, etching snakes and diamonds of Urdu verse. Hasan looked closer at the words and his faltering Urdu took flight; his brain translated the words into English, while his heart beat in time to the original metre.

Though tyrants may command that lamps be smashed,
in rooms where lovers are destined to meet,
they cannot snuff out the moon, so today,

112

nor tomorrow, no tyranny will succeed,
no poison of torture make me bitter.

Wall-to-wall poetry, Hasan thought. This could be the newest craze in interior design.

When Salman Mamoo had covered all three walls with poetry he reached up to the chinks in the far wall, and beckoned. Wisps of memory, deep blue and silver, floated in. Salman Mamoo caught them by the handful, rubbed them between his palms into strands, and wove the strands together. When he was done, his carpet of memories covered the prison floor completely and he sank his feet into it and wriggled his toes.

Ami withdrew her hands from Hasan's eyes, and her voice fell silent. Hasan felt as though he could sing again. At last he had the images to think of Salman Mamoo without imagining rats and rancid meat and the stink of sewers.

'You told me it wouldn't happen,' he said to Ami. 'You told me he would just remain under house-arrest for a while.'

It was only that there was space for the first time. Space to say and think things, knowing that the answers would be bearable. But Ami held the coffee-cup against her cheek and closed her eyes for longer than a blink. 'I know, *jaan*. I told myself that, too. We all did. I don't know . . . perhaps we were all just acting in self-defence, insisting that he would be all right, that we would be all right, just so we needn't contemplate the alternative.' She put down the cup and pressed the base of her hands against her temples, but Hasan couldn't tell whether she was trying to keep thoughts in or out. 'But if you don't think about the alternative you can't do anything to prevent it from happening. So maybe if we had thought about it, faced the possibilities, we could have done something, good

God! we could have tried. But not even to have done that much.' Ami's voice trailed into silence, then gathered itself up to its full power for a final burst. 'God, this coffee is revolting!'

It was a sign, Hasan decided. Not the coffee; the talk of considering possibilities and preventing them from happening. He left Ami pouring coffee down the sink and went to his room to find Yorker.

'All right,' he said, placing his forehead against the shiny red of Yorker's cranium. 'Let's transmit thoughts.' He shut his eyes so tight he could hear them squeezing smaller and smaller, and silently asked, 'What's the worst thing that could happen to Salman Mamoo?'

Yorker's answer: 'He could die.'

'Right,' Hasan said, standing up and opening his eyes before the words could become pictures. 'We have our quest, squire Yorker. We have to defeat Death, or at least deflect it away from Lord Salman Mamoo. Make preparations!'

Yorker was clearly in a period of rebellion, chaffing against his role as squire, so Hasan had to forage around for quest equipment himself. Rope from the storeroom, in case of unexpected mountains; pine-cone talisman to ward off bad luck; magnifying glass and lens from old glasses to use with the sun's assistance for lighting fires (the lens was from a pair of dark glasses which seemed somehow wrong, but such were the shortcomings of living in a house of people with 20–20 vision); a map (actually blank paper upon which directions would magically appear when needed); seashells and marbles for bartering; and a backpack, because Yorker refused to carry any equipment himself. Hasan ran an eye down the checklist. Just one thing missing.

Aba's voice carried down the hallway. 'A boon, sire,' Hasan

cried out, charging out of his room and falling before Aba on bended knee. 'I crave a boon.'

'Tell us this boon, fair cuz, that we may say "why, aye" or "nay".' Aba bent forward and whispered, 'Iambic feet with internal rhyme. Not bad!'

'Your sword, sire. For I fear mine was shattered in slaying the Beast and despite thy promise thou hast not bought me another.'

'Yes, well, Beasts are expensive these days. All right, here you go.' Aba produced his penknife key chain and slipped the keys off the ring. 'Be careful, the blades are sharp. Wound yourself and I revoke your knighthood. Where are you going anyway?'

There was only one place to go under the circumstances. Hasan needed to know more about Death, and his personal font of knowledge regarding the inexplicable was Merlin, who, for all his eccentricities, read a great deal and could always predict the result of a cricket match before the first five overs were bowled.

The journey was treacherous. First Sir Huss had to leave the palace unobserved to escape detection by spies. Not that he mistrusted any member of the royal family, of course, but he had to be wary of the newly appointed royal cook who never ate onions. What could that mean, except that he didn't want anyone to smell his approach? Sir Huss avoided the main portcullis and took leave of the palace through the windows of the minstrel's gallery. All was going well, and though the mountains between the palace grounds and Merlin's land would daunt most travellers, Sir Huss had traversed the peaks before and knew the safe paths. But wait! A dragon prowled across the peaks, its colour changing to meld with bush and scrub. The dragon halted in a patch of sunlight and began to perform push-ups, showing off the scales and strength of its forearms. While it was intent on admiring itself Sir Huss and his squire scrambled over the peaks, choosing speed over stealth, and descended into Merlin's land.

But the dragon had reminded Sir Huss of his greatest ally, Merlin's daughter, the Wizard (Ms) Zed, who feared nothing except dragons. Sir Huss looked up at the Wizard's balcony. She had her back towards him and was making use of her favourite magic device, The Fowne. Sir Huss was about to call out to her but stopped, seeing her tilt her head to one side and tuck a strand of hair behind her ear. Sir Huss scowled. Despite her powerful magic, the Wizard (Ms) Zed had clearly fallen under the spell of the Pale Knight, Sir No-gem.

Merlin walked out into his garden, a cup of tea in one hand and a saucer in the other, and pottered from *chikoo* tree to *chikoo* tree, pausing every few seconds to look up at his daughter.

'Merlin?'

Merlin glanced around, and held up the saucer in greeting to Sir Huss. 'No, no, Merle Out. However, his apprentice, Latif the Uncle, is present and accounted for.' He looked back up at the balcony and scrunched his nose. 'Highly disturbing. No tougher lessons for parents than a-doh. Yes, *baba*, adolescence adolescence, cause of much high depression. And what? Is one side of her brain heavier than the other? Why this tilting-shilting?'

Sir Huss hooked a finger through a hole near the cuff of Latif the Uncle's *kurta*, and brought the sage's shuffling steps to a halt. 'I have to ask you something.'

'Oh, I sense a leap into the deep complexities of life. Well then, let me wear the oracle monocle.' From his pocket the Uncle produced the monocle-frame which he carried every-

116

where with him, and held it in front of his right eye. 'Okay, fire away, but don't forget to aim first.'

'How can I help someone escape death?'

'Escape is OOQ.'

'OOC? As in DICOOC? Out Of Country?'

'No, no. O-O-Q. Out Of Question.'

'Oh.'

'Avoidance, however, might be achieved for very many years.'

Sir Huss and Yorker looked at each other and telepathically agreed that half a loaf was better than none. Unless the loaf was stale, of course, in which case rice was a better option. So Yorker thought, but then he had no teeth, and was still acting grumpy about the mundanity of a squire's life besides. So start a trade union, Sir Huss advised, and returned to the matter at hand.

'All right,' he said. 'That'll do. How do I avoid death?'

Latif the Uncle shook his head. 'Look Lancelittle, I told you once to avoid bad eyesight by eating carrots. You became Bugs Bunny with the eyes of a hawk. I told you to avoid bad skin by rubbing lemon-juice and salt on your skin. You stole all the lemons from my tree, and look, your skin glows like a worm.'

'Worm?'

'Glow worm. I told you to avoid cavities by brushing your teeth often. You didn't listen and your dentist took a trip up North with the money he billed your parents for.'

'I know all that, Unc . . . Latif the Uncle. That's why I'm asking you about this now.'

'But Huss, I could say all that because the oracle monocle told me what causes bad eyesight, bad skin and cavities. But where death is concerned the OM is as clueless as a parachute.

Do not question the simile. So, point being, before you can try running-shunning from Big-D, you must find out what causes it.'

'And how do I do that?'

'Question one who has come close enough to it to know its nature. Question the OM.'

'Oracle Monocle?'

'*Yaar*, *bachoo*, you are a tortoise on the uptake today. The Oldest Man, Huss. The Oldest Man.'

Chapter Fifteen

Even his lips were wrinkled. His skin was so leathery bees snapped off their stingers on it, and his eyes were so deep-set their gleam resembled torch-beams signalling for help from the bottom of a pit. A single strand of white hair circled his head like a halo, but surely no angel would belch so loudly. He had lived in this hammock between two palm trees in the back garden of the Pink Mansion for as long as anyone could remember, since before the Pink Mansion was pink, and no shuffling around of its tenants ever affected him.

Sir Huss had to cross the vast, pitted expanse of the Wrode to reach him, looking carefully left right left before setting out on the perilous crossing. Despite his precautions, a horse, its flesh obscured entirely by green armour, galloped along the Wrode at a pace so furious Sir Huss had to leap out of its way. Sir No-gem, he recalled, had a green armoured horse. Sir Huss narrowed his eyes. Perhaps his quest would need to be delayed while he saved the Wizard (Ms) Zed from the clutches of the Pale Knight. But the green horse charged past the Wizard's gates and disappeared round the corner. Sir Huss dusted off his armour and smiled.

At the gates of the Pink Mansion, though, Sir Huss recalled that he was approaching alien soil, with its own rules. He cast off his knighthood and transformed himself into Hasan, a commoner.

Hasan walked towards the hammock bearing in hand a spotted seashell which he had picked up the last time he was at the beach. The Oldest Man received the shell with a nod of gratitude and compared it to another shell, similar in shape and design, from his collection on the grass beneath his hammock. He wagged his head with pleasure, banged the shells together, and held a shell against each ear. The gleam of his eyes lost focus, withdrew into their pits, and his hammock began to bob up-down-sidetoside as though tossing on a churning sea. When he spoke his voice was cracked from overuse.

'This,' he beckoned Hasan closer, placed the shells against Hasan's ears, and was silent for a moment as Hasan listened to the echo and roar of the waves. 'This is the way the sea sounded when we reached the horizon, my third year at sea. Such a storm, such a storm, and the sky flowing into the sea, both sea and sky reflecting each other's darkness. Thirty men on that ship, all of us throwing our weight on the port side of the vessel and still it tilted to the starboard, just inches above the water's surface. What an attack of religion we had then! But it worked. No sooner had we sobbed out one prayer than the storm clouds scattered and blew away. We thought we had been saved, until our skins blistered, bubbled and boiled and we raised our heads to see the sun setting honest-truth setting on our heads. Oh, how we rowed out of there!'

Hasan touched his hand to his forehead deferentially. He

had been loathe to part with the shell which had given him such an interesting seahorse-shaped bruise when he stubbed his toe against it, but the Oldest Man's story was recompense enough. Hasan crossed his legs, and talked with the Oldest Man of nights at sea, and how the stars shine with a peculiar brilliance in places where fewer than a dozen eyes are watching them. Finally, the Oldest Man said, 'I have heard of Salman Haq's imprisonment. I wish there were something I could do.' In response, Hasan asked the question he had come there to ask.

'It is the spirit,' replied the Oldest Man. 'When the spirit leaves, death claims you. I know this because many many years ago, as many years as there are waves in the sea, I nearly died. I was sick, sick with an illness that had no name and that killed five members of my family. One night, as I slept, my spirit tried to leave my body through my open mouth. I woke up just in time, however, and shut my mouth tight like a trap. My spirit rushed up to my nose to escape through my nostrils, but before it could do that I addressed it mentally.

'"Spirit," I said, in a voice as honeyed as a lover's. "Why would you desert me? Stay with me longer, and I will show you a life of wonder." My spirit acquiesced, and then my life began anew as we travelled together, read together, loved together. And now we are so harmoniously united, I think I shall never die.

'But I was lucky to discover my spirit, and discover its desires. It is one thing to know you have a spirit, and quite another to get in touch with it, and learn its particular characteristics. Mine, for example, dislikes mangoes, and wanted to leave me primarily because I used to eat so many. Now I never eat mangoes, but that is a small price to pay for continued life. I miss them, though – mangoes, I mean – and one day during the monsoon season, when the air is heady with rain smells, I will take an armload of mangoes, sit under a tree, and gorge myself on them. Then I will die.'

Hasan considered this notion for a moment, then shook his head firmly. 'But suppose your spirit wants you to murder or steal or . . . or do something impossible like swim underwater for two hours without coming up for air.'

'In the third case, you would leap into the sea with a snorkel. Undoubtedly Mr Snorkel was inspired to invent an underwater breathing device because his spirit demanded it of him. But as far as murder or theft goes, na! not possible. The spirit is born of the heart and the mind via the tastebuds. I must admit, I am still unclear about the role of the taste-buds, but everyone knows the choice of what-we-eat and what-not is a constant struggle between heart and mind, and of course the outcome of the struggle affects the spirit's nature.'

The Oldest Man's eyes were now looking beyond Hasan. Looking into memory, Hasan thought. Looking into wisdom. Instinctively he turned his head to follow the Oldest Man's line of vision and saw one of the current occupants of the Pink House walk towards the hammock with a tray of food in her hands. The Oldest Man lowered one hand to the ground, pressed it firmly against the grass, and tipped himself out of the hammock.

The woman set the tray on the grass. Tea, bread and *aloo puri*. Suddenly Hasan's breakfast seemed a thing of the very distant past.

The woman shifted from one foot to the other, scratching the top of each foot with the toes of the other. The Oldest Man dipped bread into his tea and chomped noisily.

'Kamal wants to raise the rent,' the woman said finally. 'So we may have to leave.' She simpered. It was definitely a simper. Aba had told Hasan he would know one when he saw it. 'Just when I learned to make tea as you like it.'

The Oldest Man grunted. 'Tell Kamal to come and see me,' he said. The woman's simper became a smirk as she walked away. The Oldest Man offered Hasan some *aloo puri*. Hasan was sorely tempted by the smell of the potatoes, but Yorker glared at him, and reminded him of Sir Huss and the single-minded nature of successful knights.

'So,' Hasan said, one finger pressing down against the tip of his nose in an effort to look thoughtful and reduce the effectiveness of his olfactory senses at the same time. 'If the spirit does not want its host body to be a murderer, why do so many murderers live long lives? Why isn't the President dead?'

The Oldest Man scooped up potatoes with a corner of *puri*, brought the food halfway to his mouth, and whispered, 'Birds!' He nodded sagely and ate.

'That's it? Birds?'

'The year my last childhood friend died I bought myself a parrot. He would sit on my shoulder, eat crackling seeds and learn to recite love poems in six different languages. If you look closely you can still see the marks of his talons on my flesh. I tell you, that bird adored me! But then I fell in love, and the parrot always on my shoulder, entrancing the woman I loved with his romantic verse, entrancing her to the point where she forgot about me, to the point where she considered my body merely a parrot-perch . . . what can I say. I sold him.'

'You didn't!'

'That's what *she* said. I never saw her again, and couldn't bear to have the parrot back because he was the cause of my lost love. But that bird kept flying after me, until finally the man to whom I sold him built a wooden cage, hung it from the topmost branches of a tree, and kept the parrot imprisoned. For years he kept that parrot locked away in a cage where it spent its time reciting poems of loss, and pecking. Pecking, pecking at the wood, until finally one day with the combined force of rain, age, parrotbeak and parrotwill, the cage broke apart. That bird hurled itself out of the cage, raised its wings to fly to me, but the wings had lost their strength, and the parrot plummeted to the ground and . . .' The Oldest Man upstretched his arm and from that height let fall a nibble of bread into the tea. 'Splat!'

'That's horrible!'

'Oh yes. Horrible. He died quoting Byron. "Childe Harold's Pilgrimage". Horrible. But my point is: there are two ways to prevent a thing from escaping you. And some cages are more durable than others. But I, for one, would rather live without mangoes than have a parrot perpetually pecking away at my insides, waiting to burst loose.'

Hasan rocked on his heels, and attempted to separate the metaphorical from the literal in the Oldest Man's words. Spirits and parrots and mangoes were all a little unclear, but it was certain that the inability to speak in straightforward terms increased directly with age.

The air Hasan breathed was thick with questions. They swarmed around him, half-suffocating him. If he closed his eyes he could see question marks slide under his eyelids, and poise above his cornea like inverted hooks. When, as now, he tried to grab hold of a question, snap it in two, it merely divided into a multitude of new questions. Of these new questions, the most burning one was: what does Salman Mamoo's spirit want? Hasan recalled the vast quantities of mango pickle

Salman Mamoo had consumed during mid-term, and shook his head.

He left the Oldest Man to what remained of his breakfast and went to see Zehra.

She was sitting on a cane chair on her balcony, feet resting atop the balcony railing, drinking chocolate milk and whistling to Ogle with all the nonchalance of one who did not need to decipher the indecipherable in order to save a life.

'Hasan? What is it?'

Hasan shook his head, scratched Ogle's ears, and leaned against the railing. When tears threatened to spill from his eyes he gritted his teeth against them and reminded himself that he was a knight.

'Look,' Zehra said. 'I love Uncle Salman too, okay?'

'Then why are you whistling?'

'I'm not. I'm coping.' She passed him a box of tissues. 'And?'

'And what?'

'The Oldest Man?'

'Mangoes and parrots.'

'Elaborate.'

Hasan did, starting with his dream and ending with the parrot story.

When he had finished, Zehra rocked on her chair, frowning. She got up, paced the balcony, strode inside, brought out a piece of paper, scribbled frantically, asked Hasan to repeat certain parts of his tale, drew arrows connecting words to each other on the page. 'Hmmm . . .' she said.

'Hmmm what?'

'Hmmm . . . I have no idea what this means. Wid!' She darted inside, and was back a few seconds later, dragging in the Widow in by her sleeve.

The Widow arched an eyebrow at Hasan. 'Been conversing with the Oldest Man, have you?' Hasan quickly ran through the possible titles he could give the Widow. Sorceress. Queen. Damsel in dist . . . hardly! In a flash of inspiration he chose 'the Widow'.

'Yes,' he said. 'About Death.'

'Wonderful how you can say it as though it were capitalized. DEATH!' The Widow smiled. 'It's just death, you know. Just a change in location. A movement from this world to the land bordering sleep. Have you studied Venn diagrams in school?'

That was a *non sequitur* worthy of Zehra. Hasan nodded.

'Well, imagine two circles. Life and death. Or DEATH, if you prefer. Close to each other, but not touching. And a third circle, Dreams, which intersects both Life and Death.'

'Hasan hates maths,' Zehra said. 'Do you know what the Oldest Man meant?'

'Oh, yes. He and I have discussed it often. The secret to living is to know what your spirit wants and either give in to those desires or, for shorter-term and more discomforting success, imprison the spirit.' She shrugged. 'That could be true. It doesn't particularly concern me.' She turned to leave.

'Can't you stay?' Zehra said.

The Widow shook her head. 'Khan's brought his sister to see me. I have to go.'

Zehra scowled and kicked the balcony railing. 'I hope you have nightmares tonight,' she muttered. The Widow turned, surprised. She placed a hand on Zehra's shoulder, but Zehra shrugged her off. Hasan and the Widow exchanged baffled glances.

'Know the main difference between dreams and waking life?' the Widow said to Hasan.

'I used to think logic,' Hasan said.

The Widow smiled wryly. 'Dreams wait for you.' She walked away, all fire and brilliance.

Hasan scratched Ogle's stomach for a few minutes and waited for Zehra to say something. When she didn't Hasan said, 'Well, at least we know how to avoid death. Give in to the spirit's desires.'

'Makes sense, does it?' Zehra said.

Hasan nodded, perturbed by the edge to her voice.

'Try that one out on a doctor, Hasan. Or, better still, ask the Oldest Man what it was that my mother's spirit wanted that she could not give it. She had me, she had my father. She had a life, Hasan!'

Now Hasan could feel his own cheeks turn red. 'Why do you always have to be the expert on loss?' he yelled. 'This isn't about your mother, it's about Salman Mamoo. I . . . he . . . you don't even remember what your mother's voice sounded like, so you can't . . . don't.' He turned away, conscious of her breath coming quick. He wouldn't have been surprised if she had hit him.

But, instead, she said in a tone so measured he knew she was close to tears, 'My mother didn't die because of some stupid mango, okay? She died because her heart stopped.'

Hasan turned back to face her.

'Why did it stop?' he asked.

Zehra took a deep breath, and exhaled into the sky. 'No one knows. The doctors couldn't explain it. She had been for a medical check-up two days before. The results arrived in the mail just after Aboo told me she was dead. I kept those results under my pillow for weeks afterwards, as though somehow a piece of paper saying she was one hundred-per-cent healthy would prove her death to be a hoax.' She changed her tone, became suddenly brisk. 'Look, maybe the Oldest Man is right. But how are you going to figure out what Uncle Salman's spirit wants?'

Hasan set his jaw. 'It's my quest. I have forty . . . thirty-nine days in which to figure it out.'

Zehra nodded, and looked old.

Chapter Sixteen

Hasan stepped on to the roof.

'Hello, home,' he said. 'Hello, water-tank. Hello, bed.' He whisked the dust-cover off his rope-bed and ran his fingers along the criss-crossed rope and wooden frame. The rope fibres were coarse against his palm as he skimmed his hand from the head to the foot of the bed, but he knew he could sleep on that mesh of rope without an itch or even a tickle. Magic everywhere on this roof-world. 'Hello, stars. Hello, pomegranate juice.' He bent down and touched the rust-coloured stain. His finger came away covered in dust. 'Hello, Azeem.' He bowed in the direction of Azeem's roof. There, that didn't seem so strange.

'Hel-lo, cricket!'

Hasan pulled his rope-bed a little closer – but not too close – to the roof's edge, so that he could lie on his stomach and watch the match in progress in the garden three houses up from the Pink House. It had been months since the garden lights last flooded that immense lawn and stumps dug holes behind creases which were demarcated by invisible lines running between pebbles. When the nightly matches first stopped, rumour (in other words, the Bodyguard) had it that the occupants of the house had moved North and were trying to rent out their house. But no tenants were forthcoming for property which spread over two plots of land yet contained the smallest house for five miles around. It was one of those places Aba and his friends encouraged each other to rent, saying 'Yaar, who needs spare rooms and extra bathrooms and please what's the point of having both lounge and drawing room? Come on, just think of all that outdoor space for cricket.' But no one was willing to take on the house's contradictory mix of increased social responsibility and reduced living quarters, so the owners had moved back just yesterday.

The mango tree which somewhat obscured Hasan's view of the pitch had been cut down last week; the Bodyguard avoided laughter and shrill argument; and even the breeze conspired to enhance Hasan's viewing pleasure – it blew south-eastward, carrying the sounds of leather and willow straight to Hasan's ears. The batsman misread a slower delivery, charged out of his crease to hit it, and was stumped. The bowler and wicketkeeper danced towards each other, snapping fingers and holding arms aloft. Hasan grinned and felt a relief so overwhelming he could almost taste it. Nights stretched before him with a promise of constancy.

So . . . Hasan bit his lips and attempted calculation. If the day's play started at six, as it had always done in the past, and went on for five hours, at which point Hasan would fall asleep, that left nine waking hours to fill with activity. Subtract the hour spent at lunch and dinner, and that left about eight hours, plus . . . no, minus an hour watching a recording of the previous night's 'Drama Hour' on television. Seven hours. Minus breakfast with Uncle Latif plus tea with Zehra. No, minus breakfast minus tea. Or, breakfast plus tea minus . . . what was it? Seven or eight hours?

'Or, I could just spend the whole day doing maths,' Hasan said aloud.

A new batsman was walking towards the crease, bat in his left hand, his jaunty step as familiar as Ami's scent of paint and perfume and apple shampoo. Without thinking Hasan puckered his lips and whistled the whistle heard on cricket grounds across the nation. Wooo-wu-wooo-wu. Razz-le Dazz-le. The whistle's trajectory cut through opposing wind direction and carried to the batsman's ears. Raza Mirza looked up to see where the sound originated, and flashed Hasan a two-fingered sign of victory. His teeth, Hasan noticed, did not gleam.

'We have to have a serious talk.'

Hasan jumped at the voice. Aba hardly ever disturbed him up here. And even when he did, the family's unspoken rules had it that this was Hasan's territory, as sacred as Ami's studio or Aba's crossword-chair, and Hasan's whims were law. The other unspoken rule, of course, was that Hasan really wasn't allowed any whims of which Aba or Ami disapproved, but surely he could ban serious talks about subjects unrelated to cricket and expect to be humoured.

'About what?' Hasan said, in a tone meant to convey irritation and disapproval.

'Your garb,' Aba said, coming to sit on the edge of the bed. He ran his eyes along Hasan's *kurta* and jeans. 'I mean, if you will persist in this mismatch you should at least be prepared to back it up with a five-minute oral report on the advantages of being hybridized.'

131

'Inner or outer,' Hasan said, moving up to allow Aba room to lie down.

'Hmmm? Oh, you mean internal or external hybridity? Nature versus nurture sort of . . . why this expression?'

'I thought you said a report on Hebrides.'

There was the laugh. Hasan watched the backward fling of Aba's head and the dimples in his cheeks like full-stops marking an end to all unpleasantness, and thought, not for the first time, that he would give up all his outward resemblance to Ami and Salman Mamoo if he could only inherit Aba's laugh. Yes, he would even give up the promise of high cheekbones.

'When can I come and see you in court again?' Hasan asked, while Aba gulped in air.

Aba's dimples vanished. 'Well, Huss, I thought you realized . . . I mean, I don't really do that any more.'

'Do what?'

Aba looked down at his right hand. The corner of the bedframe had cut into his palm and dissected his curving life-line. 'The firm thought . . . that is, we know . . . we were told there are judges who think it is impolitic to rule in my favour, so I'm back to doing the chamber law thing. Have been for a while now. It's a nice change, really.'

Hasan moved his arm so that it touched Aba's sleeve. Across the street the bowler charged up to the bowling crease, a long run-up of incredible speed. The ball struck the pitch and reared up sharply. 'Duck!' Aba and Hasan cried out together. But Razzledazzle had picked the ball and moved his feet backward before the grass flattened in front of him. As the ball rose up to crush his skull, he raised his back foot high off the ground, brought the bat up to shoulder-height, pivoted around on his front foot and struck the ball sweet and true. The fielder at square leg boundary could only gape as the ball zipped past him, smacked against the wall and ricocheted back on to his shin. There were cheers and whistles from balconies all around. Aba closed his eyes and inhaled through his nose, as though he could smell the shot.

'You're the Razzledazzle of law,' Hasan said. 'You're razzmatazz in the courtroom.' Aba slung an arm across Hasan's shoulder and, for once, seemed to know that words would not do.

Ami's slippered feet padded up the stairs and towards the bed. She crossed in front of the bed and sat down, her back leaning against the wooden frame, and rested her head between Hasan and Aba's shoulders. 'What brings you here, woman?' Aba growled.

Ami's eyes followed the bowler's arm and Raza Mirza's shifting grip on the bat. 'The aesthetic of men's wrists,' she smiled. She reached backwards and circled the jut of Aba's wrist bone with her index finger.

'Where's Gul Mumani?' Hasan asked.

'Did you hear about the General?' Ami said.

Hasan nodded, 'Uh-huh.' He had woken up this morning to high-decibel comments of outrage regarding the nerve of the General. Precisely which general had provoked this outburst it was hard to gather, but whoever he was he wanted to hang Ami in his drawing room. That's what he had said over the telephone, 'I have had to go through great pains to get your number. But I persisted because really, truly, I would like to hang you in my drawing room.' Just like that. Ami hung up, of course, but the General called back, saying, 'Not you in person, of course, madam. I refer to the extension of your soul. Your art, that is. I wish a painting.' When Ami hemmed and hawed, trying to turn her back on Aba who kept dashing into her vision with a wagging finger reminding her how often she had cautioned him not to antagonize the wrong people, the General said, 'Now, madam, I know my fellow officer has some disagreement with your brother, but come now, doesn't Art transcend Politics?' Ami ended the conversation on the pretext of having to save her son from an enraged cockroach, and the General said he would call back the next day for details of price and delivery.

'So are you going to sell something to him?' Hasan asked.

'What do you think?' said Ami.

'Well, if you do, it shouldn't be one of the nicer ones. Maybe the new one in your bedroom.'

'Oh God, an eleven-year-old critic. Too abstract, huh?'

Hasan pulled his lower lip thoughtfully. 'The brush strokes are nice, but . . . too much green.'

Ami tipped her head backward and looked at Aba. 'Remind me why we decided to teach our son honesty?'

Aba didn't smile. 'What have you decided about the General?' he said.

Ami put a finger to Aba's lips and turned back to the cricket match. Razzledazzle had been languishing at the non-striker's end for an entire over, and now that he was finally facing the attack again he patted the ground repeatedly with the bottom of his blade like a bull pawing the ground. The ball was ever so slightly short-pitched. Razzledazzle moved his back foot across and used it as a pivot, his blade flashing and *thock*! Hasan didn't even bother to see where the ball would land; his eyes stayed on Razzledazzle as the batsman's body swung clockwise in the follow-through to complete a half-circle. 'Poetry,' Ami murmured. Hasan closed his eyes for an instant replay in slow-motion. Salman Mamoo, he was sure, was thinking of cricket now, passing the time with images of cover-drives, sweep-shots and square-cuts.

'What a pull shot!' Aba exalted.

'Oh, dodo, that was a hook shot,' Gul Mumani said, her face red from the exertion of climbing spiral stairs. In her hands was a rolled-up painting. 'Like this –' she swung the roll at an invisible ball in a motion identical to Razzledazzle's. 'See?'

'That it?' Ami asked.

Gul Mumani nodded. Ami stood up with a half-twisting motion of her body and caught hold of one end of the painting. She and Gul Mumani giggled and whispered to each other like a pair of . . . Hasan couldn't help but think it . . adolescents. Aba and Hasan rolled eyes at each other, and pretended to be interested only in the cricket. That pretence lasted all of three seconds.

'All right,' Aba said, turning to face the women. 'May we prevail on you to unveil the painting.' He held up a hand. 'I know. You'll say, it isn't veiled at all, but once a week I like to subordinate meaning to assonance.'

'Aba, I don't think they were going to say that at all,' Hasan said.

Ami stood still, holding one end of the painting, and Gul Mumani walked away from her, unrolling the painting as she moved. 'Ta-dah!' they said. Ami glanced down at it and exploded into laughter.

It was not Art.

Not even a distant relative.

What it actually was, was hard to say. The backdrop was black, and a sprinkling of bright colours arced across the top of the canvas. Hasan inspected the sprinkles more closely. They seemed to have been created by dipping a toothbrush in paint and running a thumb over the bristles to release the colours. At the bottom of the canvas, in the centre, was a red paw-print. Ogle's. Hasan began to laugh.

'We'll call it "Spew of One-Legged Hound",' Ami said.

'Beast,' Gul Mumani said. 'Not Hound, Beast.'

Aba shook his head, refusing to be infected by their mirth. 'You're not giving that to the General?'

'True. Not giving, selling,' Ami said. 'Oh, Shehryar, don't look so glum. No one will criticize the Emperor's new clothes.'

Aba was not convinced. 'You'd sign your name to that?'

Ami nodded. 'Proudly.' She shrugged. 'It's something. Small-scale admittedly, but it's something. Besides, if I'm tossed in jail for bad art I'll be happy to have helped set the precedent.'

Hasan shivered and turned away. He never knew, these days, what tossed-off comment could destroy the equilibrium of his mood and leave him scrambling for ideas, images, poems, even multiplication tables to fill up his mind. Below, Razzledazzle was run out in a mundane moment of miscommunication. Hasan kicked the bed-frame hard enough so that the pain would be overwhelming.

'Hasan!' Ami ran over to him and helped pull off his shoe.

'Don't give him that painting,' Hasan said. 'Please, Ami.'

'I won't,' Ami said. 'I won't.' She held him until the cricket ball flickered and disappeared and the sounds of the game became loud and then soft and were swallowed by the smell of Gul Mumani's cigarettes.

When Hasan woke up the match was over and the moon was full and low above his bed. Hasan felt something was amiss, but he was close enough to dreaming to dispel the limits reason set on his mind and know that everything would be all right if he flew up among the clouds and stars. In his imagination he had flown up many times. He had soared up on air-currents, felt the clouds cling to him, their texture that of the 'doll's hair' which street-vendors wrapped around sticks. He had reached past the clouds, his fingers through to

136

the grainy charcoal feel of the sky, and, in that most magic of moments, a shooting star had burned across his palm like a falling stalactite. Hasan tried to reach up towards the moon, but his limbs were heavy with sleep and now he was dreaming again.

Chapter Seventeen

Hasan shuddered awake. He had barely a moment to feel thankful for escaping from a nightmare which was already misting over in his memory, when he remembered – thirty-six days left and he had no idea how to discover what Salman Mamoo's spirit wanted. He squinted upward. Morning light diffused across the City and the sky seemed impossibly far away.

'Oh-ho, Rip Van!' Uncle Latif called out from Zehra's balcony. 'You missed the angels last night. Whole flock of them, leaping and looping above your head, but I shooed them away, told them not to whoosh so close or they would wake you up.' Hasan didn't even smile. It seemed entirely probable that if angels had appeared he would have missed them. He hated days that started in this manner. Blah days, Zehra called them.

'Blah blah black sleep, life is full of bull,' Hasan sang to himself as he descended the stairs. Why bull? he wondered. Oh . . . he grinned. Oh! 'Yes sir, yes sir, three bags full.' He giggled his way through the kitchen and into the hall where he collided with Aba and a very large canvas.

'Oh good, I was just coming to wake you up,' Aba said. 'Hurry and get dressed. You're going to the beach in . . .' he twisted his wrist to look at his watch and nearly decapitated Hasan with the canvas. 'Sorry. Forty minutes.'

'We're going to the beach?' Hasan said.

'You. You're going to the beach. Your friend Javed called with an invitation last night, but you were already asleep. Help me with this will you?' Hasan and Aba carried the canvas into the drawing room, where Ami was rearranging paintings on the wall for the third day in a row. Today Auntie Poops' etching of trees had displaced Ami's watercolour of wrestlers as the central canvas.

'Is it safe?' Hasan asked. 'Going to the beach? Why don't you hang up "Spew of One-Legged Hound" to see how people react?'

Ami chortled at the suggestion, moved back a few inches and pushed the frame up slightly to the left. 'Ordinarily we wouldn't let you go, but Javed's great-uncle's a general; he's organized a military convoy to take you all to the Officer's Cove.'

The world was full of generals these days. 'But we don't like military men,' Hasan objected.

'We like this one,' Ami said, removing the etching from its nail to Aba's obvious relief. 'Pass the camel painting. General Jojo. He was a great friend of your Nana's. I had a huge crush on him when I was thirteen because he could recite Urdu poetry backwards and lock eyelashes with his horse. Salman absolutely idolized him. Do we really want a camel in our drawing room? They spit, don't they?'

Hasan left Ami and Aba discussing dromedary drool and

went to change. It took him nearly ten minutes to decide whether to wear his new, five-pocket jeans for the purpose of showing off, or his old, knee-ripped jeans which would allow him to climb and slide and jump uninhibited by a fear of tearing the fabric. Uninhibited climbing, sliding and jumping won.

Zehra was in the driveway when Hasan wandered out. She was wearing her new jeans, Hasan noted. And Ami's new dark glasses.

'Are you deigning to socialize with the kids?' Hasan asked.

'You don't pronounce the first "g" in deigning,' Zehra said. 'And no, I'm coming along because Javed's brother invited me.'

'I didn't know you were friends with Omar,' Hasan said. He couldn't help but feel envious. Omar, at fourteen, was already one of the star batsmen of the Senior School.

'I'm not. But Najam is,' Zehra said, as though that explained everything.

There seemed little to say after that. Fifteen minutes of silence passed before a five-car cavalcade rumbled down the street and stopped outside the gate. Hasan could hear members of the Bodyguard exclaim and rise to their feet next door; he rushed out and motioned that all was well. The five cars turned out to be three Nissan Patrols with military licence plates, sandwiched between two trucks filled with armed soldiers. 'Festive!' Hasan muttered. A hand opened the door to the blue Nissan Patrol in the middle of the convoy and gestured Hasan and Zehra in. Hasan reached the door first, and backed up when he saw the hand belonged to Najam. Zehra pushed past him – pushed him aside, to be precise – and sat down next to Najam. Javed, and Hasan's other classmates, were calling out to him from the lead Nissan Patrol, but Hasan could tell that Najam didn't want to be in the same car as him, so he leaped in beside Zehra.

'I'm not that large,' Hasan said to Zehra, gesturing at the space she had left for him on the seat. 'You can move up a little.' Zehra looked straight ahead and pretended not to hear.

'Hey, cuz,' Najam said. He leaned across Zehra and poked a finger through the hole in Hasan's jeans. 'What? Can't Shehryar Mamoo afford to buy you new clothes now that he's no longer the big-shot barrister?'

Zehra moved, just slightly, closer to Hasan.

'You're cousins?' Rabia – one of Najam's 'crowd' – squeaked up from the row of seats behind Hasan.

'Second cousins,' Hasan said. That was the thing about Najam. He didn't have friends. He had a crowd. Omar of batting fame twisted round from the passenger seat and stared at the hole in Hasan's knee, before instructing the driver to overtake the car in front. Hasan leaned his head against the window and tried not to notice that the expanse of seat between him and Zehra had grown again.

The cavalcade zipped past the higgledy-piggledy of residential sections which turned commercial for a street or two and then reverted back to driveways and bougainvillaea and satellite dishes as though the interruption had never occurred. It was the first time Hasan had ventured further than Azeem's house since Salman Mamoo's arrest.

The City was clearly attempting to jerk back to normality. All the shops were open, making the most of the first non-strike day since Tuesday, and there were enough cars on the streets to add a background drone of honking horns to the sounds of Najam and his friends ranking teachers by coolness. Still, there was something very wrong in the City; even tinted windows couldn't keep Hasan from seeing that. Much hustle, but no bustle, Uncle Latif might have said.

Over the bridge now, and past plots of land where sprawling

houses were being demolished to make way for four-star hotels, though tourism was sharply on the decline. Past the Club; past the kindergarten with its fabulous white-flowered tree which Najam had taught Hasan to climb, years and years and personalities ago; past the financial district where yet another stunted version of a skyscraper was being constructed by a company with too many consonants in its name; past the harbour smelling of rust and fish; past pi-dogs; past beggars; past billboards bent backwards with the force of last summer's monsoons; past frying *samossas*, roasting corn, simmering *nihari*; and slowing now at a traffic light in the dead centre of Gulshan-e-Zafar, right across from the shuttered façade of ACE headquarters. The lock at the base of the shutters was not rusted, Hasan noticed, despite Gulshan-e-Zafar's proximity to the sea.

The soldiers in the truck ahead stubbed out their cigarettes and placed rifles at ready. Everyone in the car stopped talking. Omar turned the music down. All the shops were closed here, either in fear or protest or because the shopkeepers lived in nearby sections of the City which were still under curfew – Hasan couldn't decide which. Pine cones had been spray-painted on three shutters, and walls everywhere were sprayed with political slogans: *Salman, Baat maan, Terey hathon mein qoum kee jaan*. 'Salman, Understand, The country's life is in your hands'. The street was very narrow and there were tyre marks along the pavement. Men milled around a *paan*-stand – the only place of commercial activity – but there were no barefoot children to be seen running down the street, beating rubber tyres with a stick and seeing how fast they could go.

If only the lights would change.

'You'd think this area would be under curfew,' Najam muttered, looking around.

All the men at the *paan* stand had turned and were staring at the convoy, their lips and teeth stained red with betel-nut juice. One of the men pursed his lips and then spat. An explosion of red arced out of his mouth and splattered on the window by Hasan. Hasan jerked back from his red-rivuleted reflection.

'Frightened of spit?' someone at the back jeered.

'Leave him alone,' Zehra and Najam said in unison.

'Relax, Hasan,' Omar said. 'They can't do anything to us.'

The man who had spat started to look familiar to Hasan. And that other man – the one in profile, with the beard – he looked a little like someone Hasan had once seen with Salman Mamoo. The bearded man turned towards Hasan, revealing a scar running from eye to chin. Hasan shivered. No, he certainly hadn't seen him before. Unless the scar was new. And that man, the one in blue, surely, surely . . . Hasan was seized with a desire to roll down his tinted window and poke out his head in full view. The men – ACEmen, no question of it – would see Salman Mamoo's features just underlying his own, and they would raise their fists in solidarity and remember the days when Salman Haq was nothing more to them than Zafar Haq's nephew.

The lights changed.

Chapter Eighteen

The Officer's Cove was a strip of beach nestled between a semi-circle of rocks. Would-be visitors had to pass through two checkpoints to reach it, which was often the case with some of the least interesting places in the City. But when the Nissan Patrol pulled up to the cliff overlooking the Cove, Hasan decided it would be well worth his while to draw up elaborate plans involving deception, diversion and disguise that would allow him to gain access to the Cove without the aid of generals.

The water was clearer here than anywhere outside of pictures. Even from this height Hasan could see the sand beneath the water, with tiny pebbles scattered across the seabed instead of sharp-edged rocks or limb-tangling seaweed. A crab scuttled out of a hole in the sand near the cliff's base, but it was not of the purple, pincer-clawed variety that could cause so much glee when seen on the end of a crabbing reel yet was a source of terror when it zig-zagged in proximity to bare feet. No, the crab down below was almost a spider, dancing across the sand in a camouflage that suggested shyness rather than subterfuge. At the edges of the cove, where rock arms cradled the beach and prevented it from slipping into the sea, rock-pools promised glimpses of strange sea-creatures.

'Cool hut,' Rabia said. Hasan turned away from the beach and looked at the red 'hut' which would not have been out of place in the most upscale neighbourhoods of the City. There was even a satellite dish on the roof, and a garden at the back. Inside, there were two bathrooms, three bedrooms, a spacious kitchen and a large lounge with a dining table at one end. The walls were covered with paintings by Ami and Auntie Poops and the most despised man in the artists' community, known variously as 'Oh, Him!', 'Not Him!' and 'Him Again!' Hasan wondered if any of the officers realized that the model for Ami's 'Departing Man Seen Through Lattice' was Salman Mamoo.

'So you're Saira's son?'

Hasan turned to face a man who could honestly say that his hair was silver, not white. 'Yes,' he said.

The man smiled and extended his hand. 'Your Nana was a great friend of mine,' he said. 'I'm sure he would be happy to know that the ties of friendship between our two families have extended down the generations.' He released Hasan's hand and looked up at Ami's painting. 'She's captured the slope of Salman's back perfectly.' Hasan looked at the painting and remembered how it felt to rest his cheek against that back, his arms encircling Salman Mamoo's waist. He wished he could paint out the lattice. General Jojo filled his cheeks with air, and exhaled slowly. Najam came up to Hasan, and patted his shoulder. 'Come on,' he said. 'Get changed. Everyone's already in the water.' This was worse than when Zehra spoke gently to Hasan.

145

'I'm fine,' Hasan said, shrugging off Najam's hand. 'I'll be there in a minute.'

General Jojo saluted smartly and turned to join Javed's parents and their friends on the deck-chairs outdoors. Hasan stripped down to his swimming trunks in the bedroom and made his way down the half-broken steps which dissected the cliff-face, jumping off the second-last step so that he could feel his feet sink into the warm sand.

'Come on,' his classmates yelled from the sea. 'Come on, Hussar.' Hasan grinned, and pointed to a spot just behind them.

'Wave!' he yelled.

The wave was just beginning to swell, somewhere between the swimmers and the horizon, but already it was obvious that it would be a big one. Hasan started to run, his feet moving too fast to sink in the sand, gathering speed even though there was no question of sinking now that he was on the wet, packed sand, toeprints and tiny indentations of heels marking his rapid progress; the sea backed up a few inches, intimidated by the single-mindedness of his approach, but it could not withdraw fast enough and Hasan's feet were moving through water, trying to outpace the chill, leaping rather than running now, until the water reached halfway up his calf, and then he dived in, buffeting aside the water with his arms. The wave kept growing. Just ahead of Hasan, Javed lifted his head out of the water just long enough to contemplate the size of the wave and yelled, 'Oh, dung!'. He turned and began paddling back to shore, Rabia and Ali and Ayesha following.

Najam was a few feet ahead of Hasan, Zehra beside him. Hasan stopped swimming and trod water. This was where he would meet the wave. It was a vast wall of water now, gloriously terrifying. All the swimmers turned their backs on it, but

146

kept their heads swivelled so they could watch its approach. Through the corner of his eye, Hasan saw Najam, and then Zehra, leap up and forward into the wave as it arced above them, and at that instant he knew Najam had chosen the perfect spot, because just after they leaped the crest of the wave dipped. Now it was bearing down on him, and Hasan leaped but he was rolling, not riding, rolling beneath the water, his body tossed around, water entering nose and mouth and everything and the noise of the world disappeared; there was only a sensation of helplessness and flailing arms and the impossibility of knowing if he was near the shore or somehow being pulled in the opposite direction and was that a leg or a turtle or a pebble that hit him and suddenly there was air again.

Hasan coughed and expelled water. Nearby, Omar was doing the same. Hasan stood up, rubbed the sting out of his eye and leaned his head to one side, pounding his left ear with the flat of his palm to eject water from his right ear. Zehra and Najam were already swimming back out to meet the next wave, flushed with the triumph of being carried all the way to shore on the crest.

'Well, at least you did better than me,' Javed said. 'Come on, Hussar, we'll ride the next one.'

Hasan shook his head. His teeth were chattering. 'I need food first.' He ran his tongue along his lips. 'But nothing too salty.' He trudged back up to the hut, waving off Ali and Ayesha's invitation to join them in a walk to the rockpools. He procured a slice of fruit-cake from the kitchen, and hoisted himself on to the bonnet of a Nissan Patrol. The bonnet was hot beneath his legs and calmed his shivering immediately.

'Oh, here it is!' Hasan whispered. He leaned against the windshield, and breathed in the sea. He recognized the mood of the moment immediately; it was the same one he had found in Salman Mamoo's garden at dawn when Azeem's fall had been the most unfathomable thing in his life: the mood which allowed memory without pain.

A few months earlier – yes, it didn't hurt to think this – Hasan had been at another City beach, sitting on the terrace of Aba's firm's beach hut, drinking a cup of tea just hot enough to cut the chill of the first winter breeze. The sky had been merely blue straight ahead of him, but when he swivelled his eyes to the right he saw clouds and, through a chink in one, the sun. At first the sun was golden, bordering on white, and Hasan could look straight at it without squinting. Rays of light slanted into the water, and a filigree of gold stretched across the horizon. Hasan wished the grown-ups inside the hut would stop arguing so that he could better hear the waves providing a soundtrack for the sunset. For a moment the clouds obscured the sun completely; then the chink reappeared and the sun was flame-red.

Ordinarily, nothing would have distracted Hasan from the final minutes of sunset, but that day his eye caught something dark move across the water. Visible one moment, then gone. 'Seaweed,' Hasan said to his teacup, and then he glimpsed it again.

'Salman Mamoo!' he yelled. 'Quickly!'

Almost instantly Salman Mamoo was beside him. 'What? What is it?'

'Watch. There's something out there. I saw it twice. Wait, it'll reappear.'

A flash of tail, an arc through the air, and back it knifed into the water. 'Oh wow!' Salman Mamoo breathed. 'Saira! Sherry! All of you! Black dolphins!'

A whole school of them, suddenly, everywhere. Their backs arching through the waves, sometimes two in tandem, one just behind the other so they looked like one dolphin, extra long; sometimes one leapt a little higher and its tail broke free of the water. Just when Hasan thought they were gone, one would rise from the waves again, and again, until sea and sky were dark and the dolphins were still darker forms rising through the phosphorescent waves. When Hasan thought of dinner and looked away, they disappeared.

A few weeks later, during mid-term, Hasan was sitting on the branches of a mango tree in Salman Mamoo's garden, when Salman Mamoo hoisted himself up beside Hasan. 'Good place to talk without worrying about wire-taps,' he said. 'This must all be very mystifying to you.'

'A little,' Hasan said. 'Why exactly is everyone so worried about the military? I mean, I know the President isn't nice, and he's put you under house-arrest and all that, but what's he going to do? I mean, why is everyone so scared?'

Salman Mamoo plucked a leaf off the branch, and started poking holes into it with his fingernail. 'Remember the dolphins?' he said. 'Yes, of course you do.' He looked up at the sky, and pointed out Orion's belt, but today Hasan wasn't interested in constellations. 'Watching the dolphins, Hasan, I felt I could believe in magic, and I understood why I believe in God, but only later did I realize why the moment seemed so important. See, Huss, it wasn't the dolphins. It was the way everyone reacted to them. I don't know if you were paying attention to the conversation inside the hut just before you called me outside . . .

'Everyone was yelling at each other.'

'Yes. It was one of those things. There were eight people, and nine points of view in that room and dammit each one of us could yell our point of view as loudly as anyone else! But then the dolphins swam into sight and – remember this? –

suddenly everyone was in agreement. Standing on the terrace, looking out of the door, the windows, all of us, all so awed and moved by those – let's face it – fish, that for a moment arguments seemed impossible. How could we disagree about anything, or raise our voices in anger at each other, when we had stood together seeing dolphins leap against a sunset?'

'Things did get quiet after that,' Hasan concurred. 'But dolphins are mammals, not fish.'

'Well, that's a relief,' Salman Mamoo laughed. 'I can maintain my low opinion of fish.'

'Are you trying to not answer my question?'

'No, no. All countries need dolphins, Hasan. But the General, our self-exalted leader, well, I've seen the way he operates. If he saw people in a hut drawing together to view a dolphin, he would shoot the dolphin dead. Then he'd plant clues to suggest to each person that someone else in the hut had pulled the trigger, and when the accusations turned to violence and everyone was intent on ducking and throwing punches, he would sneak out and sell the carcass for a handsome profit. The worst part is, before long some of the people in that hut would become dolphin-killers themselves. And Huss, I don't think I could live in a world without dolphins.'

Hasan jerked upright on the car bonnet. That was it! Salman Mamoo's spirit wanted dolphins. But – Hasan's eyes swept across the still water – but if the President killed dolphins and created dolphin-killers, then for Salman Mamoo to live . . .

Zehra hopped on to the bonnet beside Hasan. 'Hey, lonesome,' she said.

'Oh, God!' Hasan moaned, slumping forward. 'Someone's got to depose the President. Someone's got to depose him within thirty-six days.'

Chapter Nineteen

Hasan moved through the darkness with eyes shut and arms parallel to his torso. His big toe stubbed against a potted plant which should have been at least five feet away from him. There was a time when Hasan could have walked blindfolded through the drawing room with all its breakables and sharp-cornered tables, but now he couldn't even negotiate his way through the hallway successfully. Four steps from the door should not have taken him to the plant, unless . . . I guess I last tried this a shoe size ago, Hasan thought. Back then, this had been just an amusing exercise to carry out in the serenity of a two a.m. house heavy with sleep while Hasan was wide awake with the excitement of being wide awake at a forbidden hour. He was tempted to extend his arms and feel his way around, but that would be giving up. He stood still for a moment and listened. The tremble of blinds in the hallway and the rustle of dining room curtains oriented him again. He remained motionless until he could feel the air currents crossing each other beneath his fingertips, remained motionless until he was so confident in his sightless seeing that he could have taken a felt-tip pen and circled the places where moonlight from the blinds' slits dappled his body. The musky scent of *Raat-ki-rani* wafted in from the garden, making the breeze seem heavier than it really was. In silk pouches of air, here and there, the smell of Gul Mumani's unsmoked cigarettes wreathed and swirled.

Hasan walked in a diagonal into the dining room, eyes still shut, and made his way around the dining table without so much as brushing against a chair. He walked around the room five times, in ever widening circles, and successfully avoided walls, paintings, furniture, curtains. At last he stopped, paused a moment, stepped forward, and felt his fingers close around a candelabra. He smiled and kissed the cold silver of the candelabra. A hardened trickle of wax tickled his lower lip. If word got out about his plan to depose the President, and soldiers broke into the house to arrest him under cover of darkness, Hasan would know how to find his way around the house in stealth and seek out objects that could serve as defence weapons.

Hasan opened his eyes and placed the candelabra back on the cabinet. Only problem, of course, was that he really didn't have a plan to depose the President. That moment at the beach when the word 'depose' came to his mind now seemed like a moment of incredible clarity. Not that it had felt that way at the time, of course. The moment between recognizing what needed to be done and realizing the weight of that recognition had been so brief that it was only in the freeze-frame of memory that he could bow his head before the splendour of the moment and hear, in the background, a sitar string shiver.

Hasan had intended, of course, to tell Ami and Aba about his revelation, even though Zehra had told him that a *coup* was obvious but impossible and he should just stop thinking about it. Every night Hasan went to sleep assuring himself, tomorrow, at the right moment, I'll tell Ami and Aba. But ten days had passed since the beach and the right moment still showed no signs of appearing. Instead, Hasan's declaration of resolve to topple the government became part of the Unsayable which adhered to every surface around the house like gummy motes of dust. Always before, conversation had cleared the air. When Hasan missed Sports Day because of chicken pox, when Waji who couldn't tie his own shoelaces accused Hasan of stealing his frog-shaped eraser, when the Widow received her first death-threat, even when Salman Mamoo was placed under house arrest, Ami and Aba had had the words to unclench Hasan's stomach.

But now his stomach was growling. Hasan wandered into the kitchen to see if there was any ice-cream left in the freezer. He pulled the freezer door open and it was like opening an alien vault which beamed out an eerie glow and froze intruders with a glacial blast. Aliens, it appeared, did not store ice-cream in their vaults.

Ice, Hasan thought. Unmanageable topics were like huge blocks of ice, so cold they burned you when you tried to handle them. But Ami and Aba knew how to lift the block with words, and with words toss it back and forth between each other, until Hasan forgot the block and clapped his hands at the twist of wrist with which Aba sent the block flying and at the backward arc of Ami's arm as she caught the over-throw. Now, however, everyone was walking around the ice, hoping it would melt of its own accord. Twenty-six days to the trial. Hasan looked at his dual digital-analogue watch. Twenty-five days.

Salman Mamoo's tea. Hasan slapped a hand against his

skull. How could he have forgotten about it? He reached into the freezer and began to push aside the plastic-wrapped hunks of meat on the top shelf. There it was! Hasan pulled out a plastic container and held it up triumphantly. Salman Mamoo's tea. He would heat it and drink it, and it would infuse him with ideas and inspiration. Hasan peered closer at the container. He opened the lid and looked inside. Frozen chicken broth. He placed the container back in the freezer and began to search again. Maybe Atif-Asif-Arif had moved it to another shelf. Hasan moved down to the second shelf, shifting bags of meat and containers of precooked food first to one side, then to the other. He squatted down and rummaged through the third shelf, his fingers crossing from numb to burning and still nothing. Nothing in the ice drawer at the bottom either. He must have missed it. He started back at the first shelf, taking each object out of the freezer and setting it down on the kitchen cabinet, his fingers red and raw now, pull out and place down, pull out and place down, pull out and place down, little drops of water dripping down the sides of the chicken-broth container, pull out and place down, pull out and place down, Hasan's fingers brushed against the water droplets as he set down a piece of steak and his fingers froze on to the next packet of meat he tried to remove. He pulled his fingers off and a tiny piece of skin stayed on the plastic. Hasan grabbed two dishcloths from a cabinet drawer, wrapped them around his hands, and went back to his job. Pull out and place down, pull out and place down. Finally, after squatting down to clear out the ice drawer, he rocked back on his heels and swore out loud. He kicked the ice drawer back in its place and leaned against the kitchen cabinet, elbows on his knees, head buried in his hands. He shook the dishcloths off his hands and sucked the bleeding finger on his hand, holding his other hand under his armpit for warmth.

Suddenly he wanted, wanted so badly his heart grew to twice its size just thinking of it, wanted to turn the doorknob to Ami and Aba's room and crawl into their bed as he had always done when fever or nerves about the next day's cricket match fought off sleep. Wanted Ami and Aba's intersecting breaths to cradle him into dreams of clear night skies and just-ripe mangoes.

It wouldn't happen. Sleep had, of late, become the great divider in the house. At any moment of the day someone was asleep, falling asleep or just waking up, and this more than anything else made these days even stranger than the first days after Salman Mamoo's arrest. Personally, Hasan had no trouble falling asleep at eleven p.m., or even earlier if the cricket match down the street ended before the allocated time. Staying asleep though was another matter. He glanced down at his watch again. Two-thirty. Usually he managed to sleep until at least four, but the nightmares tonight had been worse than ever before. Ami's light had been on in her studio when Hasan had climbed down from the roof, but when he peered in through her window and saw her staring at a blank canvas, her fingers curled into her palms, he backed away before she could see him. She would stay there until about four a.m., he knew, and if he was back up on the roof at that time and the wind direction was right he would hear the drag of her feet as she closed the door leading outside and retreated to her bedroom through the other door.

Aba, of course, saw his ability to sleep as per routine as a blow against the government, a refusal to be tyrannized within the confines of his home. So at eleven-thirty every night he would get into bed, set his alarm for seven-thirty and count words until he fell asleep. 'A, aardvark, aasvogel.' Aba claimed 'ad–' words were unfailing soporifics, but most mornings his eyes were bruised with exhaustion and when he returned from the office he slept, without words, until dinner. As for Gul Mumani, it was impossible to tell if she slept at all. Sometimes Hasan would find her in the television room, sitting upright, with eyes closed. She might stay that way for up to two hours, and just when Hasan was convinced she was asleep, a tear would slide out of her eye.

Somehow, though, guests who dropped by after dinner always commented on how well the family seemed to be dealing with things. 'It's good you remember there's still hope,' some friendly soul would say, and last night Aba replied, 'It's the hope that's killing me.'

Water dripped down Hasan's back. He shifted to the left and twisted his neck to look up at the cabinet top. Bags of meat were sweating. The thought of moving all those packages back into the freezer was too exhausting to contemplate. He leaned back against the cabinet and thought of dolphins.

There was a gentle tapping on the door leading outside. 'Hello fellow,' Uncle Latif's voice whispered from the other side of the door. 'Open sesame seed.'

Hasan pushed himself off the ground and unlocked the door. Uncle Latif stepped inside, dressed in a bathrobe and a blue and yellow polkadotted tie. 'I peered down from my balcony, but you were not on the roof. And then I saw this glow from the kitchen and said, oh my, either the Widow's husband has come to visit, and got the wrong address, or my friend Hasan is cooling himself on this warm night by using the freezer as an air-conditioner.'

'I was looking for ice-cream,' Hasan said.

'If I ever write my memoirs that will be a wonderful title,' Uncle Latif said. He began to refill the freezer.

Hasan picked up the chicken broth from the cabinet and passed it to Uncle Latif. 'So, if someone, you know, what's the word? hyper-ethically speaking, wanted to depose the President, how would he do it?' Hasan said.

'Hyper-ethically?' Uncle Latif said. 'Oh, I see. Fine word choice.' He broke a frozen water-drip off the roof of the freezer, dipped it in Vimto concentrate, and gave it to Hasan. 'Well, how to de-pose such a poser? Remove all cameras from his line of vision. Boot out all frogs and toadies, and leave him in a room without mirrors. Or perhaps, leave him in a room filled with mirrors.'

Hasan frowned, and sucked Vimto off the tapering icicle. The ice was smooth along the sides but its tip was sharp against his tongue and the Vimto was so sweet it warmed his mouth. He smiled at Uncle Latif. 'This is what the smallest stars taste like,' he said.

Uncle Latif closed the freezer door and sat on a stool beside Hasan. 'Yesterday, when I was in your drawing room, scraping the ice-cream carton – raspberry flavour, couldn't resist – that friend of Gul's whose hair looks as though bombs have exploded in it *phatak*! said, "Maybe the President will be assassinated." And Shehryar – I swear, sometimes I want to break the law just to have him represent me – said, "I hope not. I refuse to feel grateful to an assassin." And when H-bomb hair left he said to Saira, and okay, I was dropping eaves, he said, "Tyranny is killing our imaginations."'

Assassination? Hasan stared at Uncle Latif. Assassination? He walked over to the sink and threw in the remaining shard of icicle. But, of course. How else? How else? A trickle of Vimto formed a ring around his finger. If only I had a ring of invisibility, Hasan thought, I would follow the President everywhere and whisper 'murderer' in his ear until his conscience couldn't take it any more and he restored democracy just so that he could get a peaceful night's sleep.

Hasan rubbed the Vimto off his finger. But I don't have a ring of invisibility. I don't know how to get a ring of invisibility. Let's face it, there probably is no such thing as a ring of invisibility. He stared at his reflection in the window. If I could, would I do it? Would I kill the President?

Chapter Twenty

'Thank God you're finally home, Zed. I've realized something horrible,' Hasan said, sitting down on the grass beside Zehra, who was shelling peas for Imran. 'I prefer daytime to night.'

'And somehow the world still goes on turning,' Zehra replied, looking up from the pea-pods just long enough for Hasan to see that her day at the pool with Najam and crowd had gauzed her eyes red. Zehra was usually particular about wearing her goggles in chlorinated water. Hasan decided not to remark on the matter.

Hasan ran his thumbnail down the stitching of a pea-pod and opened up the casing to reveal three perfectly rounded peas inside. 'There's something really wonderful about this,' he said. 'I mean, it's so simple, it's moving, you know?'

Zehra raised her eyebrows. 'Oh God, you're going to turn into one of those boys who write poems entitled "For I Have Seen the Miracle Of Sunsets" at the age of sixteen and never have more than three words in a line.' Hasan stood up to leave and Zehra pulled him down. 'Hey, I'm the moody adolescent here, okay? So, what's the scene?'

The nice thing about Zehra was that she could hear four words for every word that Hasan spoke. When Hasan finished telling Zehra about the events in the kitchen the night before, and how he couldn't sleep after that until sunrise, she said, 'It's all about the way time moves when a wave pulls you under,' and her answer was so perfect Hasan bit a raw pea. The pea was strangely sweet.

'So how do you feel now?' Zehra said.

Hasan shrugged. 'Like an eleven-year-old who's sitting in the City while the President is in the capital surrounded by guards. But at night, when I read part of *The Lord of the Rings*, I really believe that I can do, you know, something.'

'Heard of Don Quixote?' Zehra said.

'Donkey Who?'

Zehra just smiled and rolled three peas out of the final peapod. 'Let's see what's on TV,' she said, standing up.

Ogle was in the television room when Hasan and Zehra walked in, gnawing at something that looked suspiciously like Hasan's cricket ball. Hasan was about to yell at the dog, but before he could do so Ogle lifted up a bandaged paw.

'What's happened to him?' Hasan cried out.

'Fight with a chicken,' Zehra said. 'Vicious thing swiped him with a claw.' She grinned. 'I've asked Imran to make chicken cutlets for dinner tonight.'

'That's sick, Zehra!'

'The revenge psychology is strong in today's society. That's why we think Hamlet is a wimp for delaying.' Zehra had an annoying knack for lifting excerpts from grown-up's conversations and repeating them with utter confidence, as though she actually knew what she was saying. Hasan opened his mouth to question her, but she forestalled him with a flick of the remote-control. The TV blared into life.

'Why does he always air his speeches when my favourite shows are supposed to be on?' Zehra moaned.

It was the President. He wasn't talking about Salman Mamoo. Zehra handed Hasan the remote-control and pointed to the green button at the top right-hand corner. Hasan pressed the mute button and, with his voice gone, the President's features seemed suddenly exaggerated. Hasan stared hard at the shine of his bald head, the hollows beneath his eyes, the boot-polish quality of his dyed moustache. Hasan looked at the President's jowls and imagined pulling down on their sag, way down to the ground, then releasing them to snap back up and slap his cheeks. The image wasn't as satisfying as it used to be.

Hasan lowered his eyelids until only a tiny slit remained open, and the President's features blurred and became porridge. He tried to superimpose Salman Mamoo's face on the President's, tried to see Salman Mamoo sitting in the television studio addressing the nation, but no matter how hard he tried Salman Mamoo's face would not come into focus. Hasan could feel the raw pea bouncing around his insides.

'Look Huss!' Zehra said. 'His hand. It's bandaged.'

Hasan looked from the President to Ogle, and back again. White bandage on left hand. White bandage on left paw. Ogle sat up, cocked his head to a side and used his back leg to scratch his right ear. The President scratched his right earlobe.

'Zehra! Did you see?'

Zehra laughed. 'So they scratched in unison. Quinky-dinky.'

The world was happening too fast, thoughts clamouring and rushing at such a speed Hasan became dizzy. 'It can't all be coincidence, Zed. Listen, just count . . .'

'Stop yelling.'

'They have the same birthday, all right? And the scar – look, over the eyebrow. They fell ill at the same time . . .'

'I was ill then too, remember?'

'And now the bandage and the scratching. Come on, admit it's strange.'

Zehra snorted in derision. 'Are you the animal side of our President?' she said, tickling Ogle. 'Oh no! Mix up! You got the human side. Help! That's why people call him a son of a bitch.'

Hasan could hear her laughing as he ran down the hall and out of the front door. The clouds had all rushed away, and the air was so dry it didn't even carry the memory of rain. Hasan slammed his fist against the outer wall of the house. The physical pain jerked tears to his eyes but he fought them down, head tilted to the sun so that any drop of liquid that escaped would be instantly evaporated. He fisted his right hand, like Aba re-enacting his favourite Shakespearean scene, and shouted in a whisper, 'You think I'll weep. No, I'll not weep. I have full cause of weeping but my heart shall break into a hundred thousand flaws or ere I'll weep.'

When he finished he felt absurd. He wandered into the garden and lay down on the just-mowed grass. Through the heat haze he watched sunset stream across the sky. Dribble of purple, diffusion of pink. Once, in such a moment, he had thrown back his head, shut his eyes and stuck out his tongue as far as it would go. Sky-purple dripped on to his tongue. He lay unmoving as the thick purple liquid slid down his throat. When he opened his eyes Salman Mamoo was sitting beside him holding a glass of pulpy plum juice.

'Do something,' Hasan whispered, his voice cracking as it hit the dry air. 'Do something.'

But no matter how desperately he paddled towards action, some current whirled him backwards. Whirled him into an eddy of spirits, mangoes, parrots, dolphins and, now, dog. But Hasan hadn't grown up by the sea for nothing. He knew it was best to go with the current while praying for the tide to change and sweep him back on course. Soon. For the moment, he found, as his feet were propelled down the street, the current was pulling him back to the Oldest Man.

But by the time he reached the Pink House he realized he had no idea how to phrase his thoughts, and decided to leave. The Oldest Man had seen him, though, and the topmost joint of one withered index finger jerked back and forth, beckoning Hasan forward.

Hasan drew nearer, grateful that the Oldest Man was alone. Hasan couldn't say what he was going to say around anyone else. Not even Zehra. But the Oldest Man was used to such peculiar visitors that nothing surprised him.

About a year ago, a university student, notebook in hand, had asked the Oldest Man, 'You're not lonely, then? Who visits you?'

The Oldest Man replied, 'Only the living.'

The student scribbled furiously in her notebook. 'So you don't believe in ghosts?'

The Oldest Man twitched his shoulders in a vague approximation of a shrug. 'I think the dead have ostracized me for shunning their company for so long. That's O-S-T-R-I-C-I-Z-E-D.'

With Hasan he was more forthcoming about his visitors.

'They are: people from my village who are new and lost in the City; people whose grandparents owe me a debt; people to whose parents I owe a debt; people who think I am a myth; people whose great-grandmothers once loved me; people who think old means wise; people who think wise means rich; researchers; and, thank you Allah, making all the rest tolerable, my friends – e.g., you.'

The researchers were Hasan's favourites. They arrived at the Pink House, still smelling of aeroplanes, having been in the City just long enough to find a translator. The Oldest Man was always gracious enough to act as though the translator was needed. No matter how often he watched it, Hasan never tired of seeing the Oldest Man 'do his act': gesticulate to the Heavens, reiterate his love for simple pleasures, and, at least twice, say, 'Have you really travelled across the waters?'

Today, though, the Oldest Man's only companion was a crow, perched on his toe, with a piece of grass dangling rakishly from its mouth. The crow nodded at the Oldest Man and flew off when Hasan neared the hammock. The Oldest Man motioned Hasan to sit down. 'So, Hasan, what is this question I can see getting ready to dive off your lips?'

Hasan shook his head. 'I'm not even sure myself what the question is.'

The Oldest Man nodded. 'Some say that is the beginning of wisdom. Myself, I call it confusion. But try.'

'Okay. When I came here last you told me about the spirit, and how someone like the President must have imprisoned his spirit. I thought that meant he must have imprisoned it inside, you know? I mean, somewhere inside him. But, you know Zehra's dog, don't you?'

The Oldest Man chuckled. 'When you live as long as I have you get used to hearing strange remarks collide together *dharam*! but that's the most interesting one this decade. You mean the black dog? The one named after the President?'

Hasan nodded. 'It was just a joke at first. Because they had the same birthday and a scar over the left eyebrow. But since then, there have been other things. They fell ill at the same time; Ogle was in a really strange, frisky mood the day Salman Mamoo was arrested; today, Ogle's left paw is bandaged and so is the President's left hand; and while the President's speech was being broadcast live on television, he and Ogle scratched their ear at the same moment. And these similarities are only the ones I've noticed. So, I was wondering, I don't know what, but I remember a couple of years ago I heard you saying something about animals being used for black magic . . . oh I don't know!'

'What are you saying? You think the President's spirit has been imprisoned inside the dog? If that is so, and you need to break open the prison to free the spirit, where does that leave the dog?'

Hasan suddenly felt very embarrassed, as though he had been caught believing in the tooth-fairy. He tore a handful of grass from the ground, and shook his head. 'I suppose it's all just coincidence.'

The Oldest Man placed a shell against his ear and lay back. 'When you play cricket you must keep your eye on each ball that is bowled your way, but you must also know which ones to leave alone, which ones to block defensively and which ones to hit over the boundary line. When you are in the last over of a championship match you may be inclined to hit everything you see, but what good will that do you? You try to hit the bouncer that you should duck under. Your bat misses it completely. The ball strikes your temple, whack! You retire hurt. You miss the chance to hit the next ball for a winning six! Goodbye happiness.'

Hasan threw his pieces of grass up in the air. The day after Salman Mamoo had been placed under house-arrest he had found his first moment of absolute calm while watching a cricket match on television. When the audio link was disrupted, shortly after the fall of Razzledazzle's wicket, and the commentator's voice disappeared, Hasan was triumphant about his ability to know exactly what was going on without any experts feeding him information about the length of the delivery and the merits of the batsman's stance. (Aba, of course, noticed immediately that when the link was restored the commentator stopped referring to the new batsman and team captain by his first name – Salman – and started to call him by his last name – Akram. This was tremendously confusing since the other man at bat had the same last name. Only when Salman Akram was bowled out did the commentator yell, 'Careless shot, Salman! Salman cracked under the pressure. Questions must arise about Salman's leadership ability.')

Trust the Oldest Man to take a game Hasan knew so intimately and talk about it in terms Hasan understood completely, yet still make little sense.

'What were you like when you were my age?' Hasan asked the Oldest Man. 'Do you remember that?'

The Oldest Man opened his eyes wide. 'Remember it? Better than today's breakfast. I, too, was full of questions then. But I was also surrounded by people who had straight answers for everything. It instilled terrible habits in me.'

I wouldn't mind some terrible habits, Hasan thought to himself, as he trudged back home, kicking a stone ahead of him. He kicked the stone all the way home, inside the driveway, through the front door and into his bedroom where Zehra was waiting for him, Ogle acting as her pillow.

'I thought you would be laughing with me. But then you disappeared,' she said. 'So, what about Ogle and the President?'

Hasan shook his head. 'Nothing. Straw-clutching. I just had to talk to the Oldest Man to clear my head.'

'That's a relief. I was afraid you would have a Hazrat Ibrahim moment. You know, something like, "God has spoken to me. Let's slaughter Ogle, and maybe at the moment of sacrifice he'll turn into the President."'

Hasan smiled. 'No, I ducked that bouncer. Hey! I finally understood something the Oldest Man said. Besides, I haven't been fitted with an audio connection to God.' He was still smiling at the cleverness of that remark when Zehra spoke up again.

'But if you had believed it? If the Oldest Man had told you there was a connection between Ogle and the President's spirit, what would you have done?'

Hasan lay on his stomach and touched his forehead to Ogle's wet nose. 'I don't know. I don't know. Zehra, I almost wish the trial were today. I just want this over.'

Chapter Twenty-One

In pockets of the world where disbelief had never tainted the air, magic was still possible. Such a pocket existed beneath Hasan's desk, though he hadn't realized it until six days earlier when, still distracted by thoughts of his conversation with the Oldest Man, Hasan had knocked a pencil beneath his desk and smelt dragons when he bent down to retrieve it.

And tomorrow it would be May. Hasan flung a blue bed sheet over his desk, making sure the edges reached down to the floor, and crawled between the desk legs. He drew his knees up to his chin and rested his back against the wall. The blue flaps of the tent slapped open, and Salman Mamoo walked in. Dusk-fairies swarmed in front of him in a mass of wings and stingers.

'It's all right,' Hasan said to the dusk-fairies. 'He's more than a friend.' The dusk-fairies sank to different corners of the tent, feebly chirping their greetings.

Salman Mamoo clasped Hasan's arm, his fingers touching Hasan's elbow. 'So . . . Sir Huss,' he smiled. 'Where are we?'

Hasan picked up the magical Staff of Kryket from atop the mass of maps strewn across the low-lying table, and handed it to Salman Mamoo. 'A place without clocks, and with no sundials that work.'

Hasan and Salman Mamoo walked out on to the field. A unicorn lowered his horn in greeting as he sauntered past. From amidst the cluster of warriors around a fire someone with gleaming teeth flashed a victory sign. Hasan pointed up and Salman Mamoo looked to the leaden cast of the sky. It was as though someone had taken a blunt pencil and scratched it over every inch of sky, and then blended the scratches together with a slightly greasy thumb.

'No one can keep track of day and night any more,' Hasan said. 'And the dusk-fairies are dying.'

A giant yellow kite swooped down towards Hasan, a boy crouched in its frame guiding the kite's movement with the dip of his shoulders. The kite skidded to a stop, and the boy hopped off. 'The Warlock's forces are amassing about five miles from here,' he said. 'But the Warlock is still in his castle.'

'If I could just bypass his armies and meet him one on one, I could defeat him and break the sky-spell,' Hasan said, hands straying to his scimitar.

'The Staff of Kryket and I are at your disposal,' Salman Mamoo said.

A voice, blurred by entry portals and magic zones, called out Hasan's name. 'I have to go,' Hasan said.

The boy shrugged. 'Time doesn't move here without you. Go, live your other life.'

Hasan strode back towards his tent, whispered the magic word 'Sirius', pushed aside the tent flaps and crawled out from under his desk. Atif-Asif-Arif hammered on the door and said, 'Are you in there?'

Hasan opened the door. 'I am now,' he said.

Atif-Asif-Arif looked offended. 'Well, your mother said if you're awake you should join her next door for breakfast.'

Hasan turned to put on his shoes, and then turned back. 'What's your name, by the way? Atif, Asif or Arif?'

'Aqib.'

'Oh.'

Hasan slipped on his shoes and wondered whether he should wake Zehra up for breakfast. It was only 6.33 a.m., and a few months ago Zehra would have thrown a heavy object at him for pulling her out of her dreams at such an hour. These days, though, she was inclined to give him a great deal of latitude in most things. Might as well take advantage of that while it lasted.

But when Hasan levered himself over the boundary wall with the aid of a flower pot, he saw that Zehra was already awake and sitting out on the terrace with Ami, Ogle and the Widow, slathering apricot jam on to a piece of toast. Hasan crawled in the mud between wall and shrubs, intending to leap out with a roar and frighten Zehra into dropping her toast within snapping range of Ogle's jaws. It was a delicate operation, requiring patience and timing. No point roaring when Zehra's hold on toast was firm, or when Ami or the Widow had cup in hand, halfway to lips, in prime droppable position.

Imran slid open the screen door from the dining room and stepped out on to the terrace with the newspaper and an envelope in his hand. 'This just came for you –' he said, handing the envelope to the Widow. 'A driver delivered it, but he's gone now.' His thumb and forefinger still gripped one end of the envelope. 'It's urgent, but not so urgent that you can't first finish your tea. I asked.' He relinquished his hold on the envelope and walked back to the kitchen, the muscles of his body conveying utter disdain for people who interrupted the sacred ritual of morning tea.

The Widow put the envelope aside and picked up her cup. Ami pushed the rubber band off the newspaper, stared at the front page for a few seconds and dropped the paper. 'Another strike today,' she said, her voice flat.

'ACE?' the Widow asked.

'Who else? They're protesting the death of three of their party men in police custody.'

The Widow set down her cup of tea. Now both cups of tea were on the table and Zehra was balancing her toast on the tips of her fingers, but Hasan wasn't feeling particularly leonine any longer.

'You sound less than supportive of the grand cause,' the Widow said. 'What would your brother say?'

'Damn my brother,' Ami said, picking up the paper and slapping it down on the table. 'Damn the whole bloody mess.' She cupped her face in her hands and began to cry. Hasan pressed himself against the wall and inched away.

The Widow, her arms around Ami's shoulder, said, 'Saira, you haven't slept properly in days . . .' and Ami started laughing in a way that made Hasan want to run. 'Oh Wid, if it were only that simple,' she said.

Less than fifteen minutes later Hasan and his cricket bat were staving off a barrage of imaginary balls in his back garden when Zehra strode into view. 'So come on, we're going,' she said.

'Go away,' Hasan said, hitting a lofted cover drive. Zehra stretched out her arm, fingers curled. 'Got it,' she yelled. 'You're out.'

Hasan rolled his eyes. 'That shot went about a zillion feet

above your head,' he said, walking towards her, bat in hand. 'And we can't go anywhere. There's a strike.'

'Hmmm . . . Thought I heard someone in the bushes during breakfast,' Zehra said. 'We're going with the Widow on a rescue mission. Some married guy died. And it's just nearby, next to Javed and Omar's house, so we won't have to cross any main roads to get there. No one will see us.'

'I'm not going anywhere. I'm observing the strike to show solidity with ACE.'

'You mean solidarity. With POTPAF. Come on, you've been dying to see the Widow in action. And your mother says you can go.'

Hasan thought again of Ami crying. 'I'll come,' he said. His step became bouncier as he approached the Widow's car. It was true, he had been longing to see the Widow chase away evil brothers-in-law for almost three years now, as had Zehra, but the Widow had never allowed them to come along with her. 'Houses of mourning are not cricket fields,' she said whenever Zehra broached the subject. 'No spectator seats.'

'So suddenly there are tickets available?' Hasan said, reaching in through the front window of the red Honda Civic to unlock the back door.

Zehra shrugged. 'Your mother asked Wid to take us. Hey, not so glum, chum,' she went on, in a perfect imitation of Uncle Latif. 'It must get tiring trying to look cheerful for your sake.'

'Yeah, well I wish she was doing a better job of it,' Hasan said, crossing his arms and leaning back against the leather seat. Khan and the Widow got into the front seats, and Hasan pressed his lips together and looked away from Zehra.

'Make sure you stick to the back roads,' the Widow told Khan.

172

'Why?' Hasan asked.

'There'll be ACEmen patrolling the streets to ensure the strike – why don't they be honest and call it a curfew? – is observed,' the Widow said.

Khan nodded. 'Their situation is getting desperate,' he said. 'They need to show the government they still have enough support to bring the whole nation to a standstill.'

'Maybe you children shouldn't come along,' the Widow said.

'Oh come on, Wid!' Zehra said. 'It'll be fine. Khan will stick to the back roads.'

Hasan tried to make sense of all this. Why was the Widow worried about running into ACEmen? And how could the ACEmen 'ensure' that the strike was observed?

Khan reversed the car out of the driveway and was greeted outside by the *putt-putt-khrr-khrr* of a rickshaw engine that seemed to be remonstrating against not having been retired to a junkyard years earlier. Actually, the engine and the rest of the wedge-shaped rickshaw had been on their way to a junkyard, years earlier, but before they reached their destination Khan had intercepted their owner with a bagful of mangoes; three days later, with the aid of yellow paint, masking tape, rubber bands, prayer and abuse, the Bodyguard had turned the rickshaw into its official transport unit. Of late the rickshaw's accelerator and brake pedals had been jamming in place when pushed with just a fraction too much force, which could explain why Mariam-the-Immaculate-Conceiver was sitting cross-legged in the driver's seat while Masood/Masooda-the-Transvestite was lying across the floorboard, hands hovering over the pedals.

'Have they ever actually protected you?' Hasan said, twisting around in his seat to watch the rickshaw with its five passengers follow Khan down the street.

'They loom,' the Widow said. 'That seems sufficient.'

Zehra's hands slapped a tattoo on Hasan's knees and, without too much faltering, she and Hasan sang out:

'Oh watch the Bodyguard loom
In a rickshaw with just enough room
To accommodate
Three whose husbands are 'late'
Plus a *hijra* and Jowly-Haroon.'

This was definitely better than being at home, wondering what the adults had been saying the second before he entered the room, Hasan decided. And it was a good thing that today was a strike and the streets were deserted, otherwise Masood/Masooda's propensity to press the accelerator each time Mariam yelled 'red light' could have had unhappy consequences. *Oh watch the Bodyguard loom*, Hasan whistled. Khan pulled up to a marble-pillared house.

'Widow, activate super powers,' Hasan said.

'Oh dear,' said the Widow, opening the car door with her little finger and a slight pressure of elbow. 'You've been listening to rumours.'

She rapped on the gate of the marble-pillared house and, when the *chowkidar* slid open the porthole like the gatekeeper in *The Wizard of Oz*, the lift of the Widow's eyebrows left him no choice but to open the gate without question and let her in. The *mali* watering the flowerbeds stared slack-jawed as the Widow strode past in her multi-hued sari of swishing silk, followed by Hasan, Zehra, Mariam, Haroon and Masood/Masooda. The remaining members of the Bodyguard stood watch outside.

'You're drowning the roses,' Masood/Masooda said to the *mali*, and threw him the burlesque of a kiss. The *mali* jumped back and slipped on a wet patch.

'We hear she is a Wiz of a Wid if ever a Wid there was,' Hasan sang. Zehra nudged him quiet, but she was giggling too.

The Widow swept inside through the front door, paused for a moment on the chequered marble floor and then walked a diagonal across black squares towards a curving staircase. There were voices drifting down from the second storey of the house, and Hasan was glad to follow the Widow up, away from the formality of the ground floor with its suggestion of air that was never gulped into or sighed out of lungs, but only inhaled and exhaled in quantities that met the minimal demands of the human body.

Upstairs, a door was slightly ajar, and the Widow pushed it open to reveal a dark-panelled room in which two men with sheafs of paper in their hands stood over a woman in an armchair. The men swung around to face the door as it groaned open.

'You!' the shorter of the two men said, taking a step towards, and then away from, the Widow.

'Did you call her here? Did you?' the other man said, his index finger slashing the air inches away from the seated woman's face.

'There was a shift in the equilibrium of things,' the Widow said, looking around distractedly, as though she had heard the men's voices but could not see them. 'It ruined my morning cup of tea. That's what brought me here.'

O-kay, Hasan thought. This is better than the movies.

'Do you know everything you should know about inheritance rights?' the Widow asked the seated woman. The taller man moved towards the Widow and at the same time, amazingly, the three members of the Bodyguard loomed. How it happened, Hasan couldn't say, but it was as though all the muscles in their faces which allowed them to smile or soften disappeared, and what remained was a tautness of jaw and single-mindedness. Masood/Masooda-the-Transvestite, Mariam-the-Immaculate-Conceiver and Jowly-Haroon, were suddenly unsuited to their playful nicknames. The only name that fit them was the one which, through overuse, had almost lost its meaning: the Bodyguard.

The tall man looked from face to face and then threw up his hands and walked towards the door.

'Fine,' he said. 'Come on, Abbas. Let her take that attitude.'

'Just a second,' said the Widow. 'If those papers pertain to her inheritance, I think you should leave them here.'

The men flung the papers at the Widow, and stormed out.

'All bluster,' the Widow said. 'The best kind.'

'Thank you for coming so quickly,' the woman said.

Now what? Hasan wondered.

'Tea or coffee?' the woman said.

That was the most exciting comment anyone made for the next half hour. The Widow declined all beverages, and then there was only the rustle of paper and the Widow's voice explaining inheritance laws, using words like 'title deed', 'twenty-five per cent', 'claimants', 'one-sixteenth', and no one even offered Hasan a Coke. At length the Widow looked up at Zehra and said, 'You can tell Khan to drop you home and come back for me.'

The two men who had provoked the Bodyguard loom were in the driveway, discussing manure delivery with the *mali*. They nodded at Hasan when he walked past them, and one of them tossed a rose at Zehra, who blushed.

So much for rescue missions.

Chapter Twenty-Two

'Well, what did you want? One of the men to draw a gun? The Widow to knock it out of his hand with a flying kick?'

'Stop acting so superior, Zehra. You were bored too. I saw you counting your split ends.'

Zehra glared at Hasan and flipped her hair over her face so that Hasan couldn't see her expression. Clearly, split ends were a touchy issue. Hasan remained kneeling on the front seat, facing backwards, his arms clasped around the backrest, intending to make his gargoyle face and surprise Zehra into laughing the instant she uncovered her face, but Khan pulled at his arm and told him to sit properly. There was an edge to Khan's voice which warned Hasan not to argue. Perhaps Khan was annoyed at having to leave the rest of the Bodyguard and drop Hasan and Zehra home. Or something.

Khan turned on to Seabeach Street, and Hasan rolled down the window and breathed in the salt air. The street sloped downhill about two miles, all the way to the sea, and trees of all varieties, including one with silver leaves, formed a canopy along the length of the street. It always seemed cooler on Seabeach Street than anywhere else in the vicinity. A beige car zipped across the intersection halfway down the street, and blocked Hasan's view of the sea for an instant. Khan slammed on the brakes.

'What? What happened?' Hasan looked side to side for a scampering animal without traffic sense.

Khan held up a hand for silence. He put the car in first gear, his foot still on the brake pedal. The beige car reversed back into sight. Khan spun the car, ninety degrees, to face a massive black gate and pressed the heels of both palms on the horn. The beige car turned on to Seabeach Street and started moving towards the Widow's car.

Trickles of sweat were making their way from Khan's hair to his beard, and his palms seemed affixed to the car horn. Hasan's teeth bit down on the finger joints of his fisted hand. There was no movement behind the black gates.

'Behind you,' Zehra yelled, and Khan screeched backwards into the gateway which had opened across the street.

'Close it, close it,' Khan yelled to the *chowkidar* who had opened the gate, squealing to a stop before he backed into the car already in the driveway.

A man, pipe in hand, was standing in the doorway to the red-bricked house. Khan got out of the car and walked towards the man and at the same instant Khan opened his mouth to speak, Hasan remembered why the beige car seemed so familiar, and both Khan and Hasan said, 'ACE.'

No doubt about it. The bump on the fender, the weblike cracks in the windshield, things Hasan hadn't even noticed he had noticed about the beige car until now, but no question of it, he had seen those marks, that car, a hundred times before in photographs, in news reports, at rallies, even once or twice in Salman Mamoo's driveway, and he had heard, and told, the tale of the car's driver: Shehzad, who once covered Salman Mamoo's body with his own when he saw the glint of sun on gun-muzzle during a rally, and so passed into legend, even though the gun was just a child's toy.

'You had better go inside,' the man with the pipe said, opening the car door. Hasan stepped out and was about to explain, Really, nothing to worry about, when he sees who I am he'll know we support the strike, but the man had already turned back to Khan. Zehra caught Hasan by the sleeve and pulled him up four grey steps to the front door of the house.

A car inched past the gate. Hasan imagined springs under his feet, and jumped up, not nearly as high as he thought the springs could take him, but high enough to see over the top of the gate and see, too, that there were three men in the beige car and one of them was Shehzad. The car engine was switched off. The car rolled back, parallel to the gate, and stopped.

The man with the pipe brushed past Hasan and opened the front door, easing the handle down one millimetre at a time and grimacing at the click of the latch as the door opened. He ushered Zehra and Hasan inside and picked up the cordless phone on a table just inside the door.

'Hello, police,' he whispered into the receiver. He flashed Hasan a smile which was obviously supposed to be reassuring, and disappeared into the next room with the phone in hand, closing the door behind him.

Hasan followed Zehra back out on to the steps leading to the driveway. Khan did not seem to be aware that they had stepped out again. He and the *chowkidar* were standing in the garden, out of sight of any eye that might peep through the crack between the two doors of the gate. Hasan thought of running over to Khan, or ducking back inside, but there was no reason, he told himself, no reason to be afraid. Outside, a car door opened. A man walked up to the gate, his sandalled feet visible between the gate's lower spikes. Khan laced his fingers together and pushed at the cuticle of one thumbnail with the tip of the other thumbnail.

Half-moons of fingernails, stars in your eyes, lightning reflexes, cloudy vision, thunderous thighs. Hasan chanted overlaps of body and sky to himself.

'What now, Quixote,' Zehra whispered to Hasan.

This was stupid. Stupider than a President's spirit trapped in a dog's body. Hasan had only to yell out, 'Shehzad, oh hey, Shehzada! Seen any good pine-cones lately?' and everything would be all right. Hasan opened his mouth. He heard, just outside, the slide of steel: a safety disabled on a semi-automatic weapon.

Zehra shrugged, and stepped into the driveway. Hasan reached out, wanted to, would have, intended to, reach out a hand to stop her, but his hands instead covered his heart, his stomach, and his body bent into a question mark, his knees buckled, his hands reached up to the back of his head, his face pressed between his knees, but now his back was exposed and so he rolled on to his side, his back against the door, body a ball, his legs shielding face and chest so that the bullets would hit knee caps, that's all, and shins maybe and oh, please, life.

Police sirens. Car door. Revving engine and the squeal of wheels on asphalt. Zehra's arms around him, and his around hers, the movement of her back muscles beneath his palms a miracle beyond sunsets.

'What's wrong, Huss? Are you feeling ill?'

180

'Zehra. He was . . . Zeh . . . Shehzad. Didn't you hear the gun?'

Zehra tugged his ear. 'Idiot. He struck a match, that's all.'

Hasan tried to stand up. 'Are you sure?'

'Not really. But that's what it sounded like. Come on, let's thank pipe-man and go home.'

On the way home, Khan said, 'Shehzad's brother was one of the ACEmen killed in police custody yesterday.' Hasan didn't reply. Shehzad, who Salman Mamoo had once called 'my right arm, and leg'; Shehzad, who was generally credited with organizing the rain of pine cones every evening into Salman Mamoo's house; Shehzad, who had proved himself willing to die for Salman Mamoo; Shehzad had terrified him.

Khan pulled up outside Hasan's house, and Hasan stepped out, then swung back to look in through the passenger-side window at Zehra. 'When you walked towards the gate and I thought there was a gun . . .' he began.

Zehra ran her fingers across his lips in a zipping motion. 'Go find your mother,' she said. 'It'll make you feel better.'

Zehra knew a lot, even for a thirteen-year-old.

Ami's studio was reassuringly cluttered when Hasan entered it. Canvases, easels, paints, brushes, books about artists, books by artists, flyers announcing exhibitions, tapes, CDs, sketch-pads, empty teacups, poems copied out in Aba's Roman-font handwriting, and an assortment of art supplies lay scattered across the floor and built-in shelves. The half-drawn rust and beige curtains framed the hibiscus tree outside. Ami was balanced, cross-legged, on a high stool, paintbrush between her teeth, frowning at the canvas before her. A white hair had appeared on her head.

Hasan came up behind Ami, climbed on to the lowest rung of the stool and rested his chin on Ami's shoulder, his arms around her waist for balance. He pursed his lips in an attempt to look profound, and was momentarily distracted by the taste of apricots on his lower lip before he turned his attention to the canvas. A man sat in a prison cell, one arm raised in a diagonal, tilting the face of a tin plate into his field of vision. A moonbeam squeezed between the bars of the cell window and expanded on to the plate, carrying with it the silhouette of a twirling dancer, the henna of her side-stretched hands gifting colour to the cell. After Hasan had stared at the painting for a few seconds it began to seem as though the tin plate was the moon, beaming light and dance on to the outside world.

'You're not going to sell that, are you?' Hasan said.

'You don't like it?'

'I don't want it to leave the house.'

Ami cupped Hasan's cheek with her hand. 'I thought I would hang it in the bedroom. Speaking of which, I got a call today from the General who wanted to hang me in his drawing room. He reiterated how much he adores the painting with "too much green", which you so clearly despised.'

'I didn't despise it. I mean, it's not in the same category as liver.' Hasan traced the form of the dancing girl an inch off the canvas. 'This one is mangoes.'

'You know the story of the Emperor Shah Jahan?' Aba said, walking into the studio and standing in front of the canvas. 'He was deposed by his son, Aurangzeb, and imprisoned in a tower. How do you survive something like that? Well, Shah Jahan embedded a diamond in the prison wall, facing the window. When he lay in bed he could see the Taj Mahal, which he had had built in memory of his wife, reflected in every surface of the diamond. That sight kept him alive for eight years.' He took Hasan's hand in his own. 'Zehra told me what happened. How are you holding up?'

Hasan found he couldn't talk about his morning in any great detail, but somehow it was enough to smell the combination of Ami's oil paints and Aba's aftershave. Or so he thought. But that night, long after Gul Mumani had finished telling Hasan the Laila-Majnoon story, and images of the madman-lover weeping hollows into stone had wisped out of his bedroom, Hasan began to shiver. Majnoon digging a grave for Laila, that was the only part of the story that would not leave him. Laila dead. The answers Hasan thought he had, the answers the Oldest Man gave him about spirits and mangoes and death, they had led him only to a Labrador with a bandaged paw, and now, no hiding from it, the truth was out: people die because of bullets and gravity and rope.

And because a President is alive to sign the execution orders.

Chapter Twenty-Three

Hasan realized, as he stared down at the blank page before him, that this was *the* Test. Yes, the one Aba had warned him about; the one which marked the point when flipping through the pages of a textbook on the way to school was no longer sufficient to ensure a comment of 'Excellent work! Handwriting needs improvement!' from the teacher.

Hasan tried to console himself with the thought that at least his handwriting would merit no complaint this time. He had copied the test question off the board with as much care as Uncle Latif took in choosing which *chikoos* to pluck off his trees. However, just as Uncle Latif's careful testing of texture, weight and colour failed to compensate for his recently developed allergy to *chikoos*, the inspired loop of Hasan's 'l' and the compass-created roundness of his 'a's failed to detract attention from the stark blankness of the page below the question: 'What made Alexander great?'

For a moment, recalling the success of his crescent drawing, Hasan was tempted to answer 'Allah' but something in the steel rim of Mrs D. Khan's glasses convinced him otherwise. All he could remember about Alexander was that he wept when his horse, Bucephalus, died. Finally, recalling Aba and Salman Mamoo's arguments about history, Hasan wrote 'Point of view'.

He leaned sideways in his chair and rested his cheek against the green-painted wall, the stone a far more effective cooling agent than the whirring fan which merely made the warm air in the classroom move faster. His fingers traced the letters scratched into the brown paint of the desk by previous inhabitants with steel rulers and sharp-tipped dividers. 'Take out the "SH . . ." from school and what are you left with? Students', 'I hate Geography', 'Geography hates you', 'A.R. and Y.H. forever', 'I rock!', 'You block, you stone', 'I wish I was a koala bear', 'Eucalyptus!', 'You calyptus yourself', 'Cricket – more than an insect.'

Pages flipping, ink smell intoxicating, pen nibs biting into paper. Thank God school had finally reopened. Poems to learn, highest test-marks to compete for (there would be a lot of catching up to do after today), cricket to play during break time, teachers to mimic, older boys with voices breaking and hair slicked back to tease Zehra about, now that, for unknown reasons, she had reverted to referring to Najam as 'that cousin of yours'.

Hasan's compass scratched intersecting circles on to the desk.

Eight. Eight. Pieces o' eight. Figure eight. Days left: eight. Ate. Eight. Next week decides if Mamoo lives or dies. Hasan started to remember mid-term, but forced himself to stop before he had even crossed the driveway and thrown his arms around Salman Mamoo. Remembering Salman Mamoo came perilously close to thinking of him in past tense. Hasan closed his eyes and mentally transported himself back under the blue-sheeted desk. He and Salman Mamoo stood before the Warlock's castle, Salman Mamoo hunched over to prevent his head from hitting the leaden cast that had thickened so much it almost reached from sky to ground now. Hasan reached up his fingers to the greyness and touched the slime-coated slate.

'Quick!' Salman Mamoo said. 'We have to get to the Warlock before his magic crushes us.'

'Time's up!'

Mrs D. Khan walked around the class collecting test-books, one end of her *dupatta* tracing letters on the floor as it trailed behind her. Hasan shut his book before she could see the blankness of his page, but when she picked up the book she balanced it on the tips of her fingers for a second, as though weighing its wordlessness. She collected Javed's book next, and his pages were so bloated with ink that the front cover would not stay closed without the pressure of a hand on it.

'Do you have cephalopods hidden in your desk?' Mrs D. Khan said to Javed, staring grimly at his book. Javed gaped, and turned to Hasan for assistance. Hasan chewed the end of his pen and looked distracted. *Trrring-trring.* 'The proverbial bell,' Mrs D. Khan said and swept towards her desk. 'Line up. Single file. Down to the auditorium, and slowly. Do we know the meaning of slowly, Hasan? Well then, let's demonstrate it.'

At the pace that Mrs D. Khan dictated, her class was the last to reach the outdoor auditorium. As befitted their status as the eldest students in the Junior School, Hasan and his classmates sauntered past Classes III, IV and V without acknowledging them before waving and mouthing greetings to the other two sections of Class VI at the back of the auditorium. The principal, Mrs Qureshi, went up on stage and cleared her throat. Hasan almost tripped over Nargis Lotia's feet in his haste to

186

sit down on one of the steel fold-up chairs which seemed designed to encourage squirming.

'My brother's friend wants your neighbour's number,' Usman Lohawalla whispered, swivelling his head around towards Hasan.

Hasan shifted in his seat and tried to concentrate on the sonorous tones of Mrs Qureshi who spoke and swayed on the stage in tempo to some untuned iambic instrument in her head. 'Due to the unforeseen and extended closure of school' – the other students darted glances at Hasan – 'we had to delay, and almost cancelled, the school oratory competition, but since the winner of the contest is to represent our school at the National Oratory Competition we felt it was important that the event take place.'

'I don't know why they bother,' Javed whispered to Hasan. 'Everyone knows you'll win. And I bet you'll win the national competition too.'

Hasan tried to look surprised by the compliment. Dragonflies were beginning to flit inside his stomach in a way that had always foretold victory.

'We have just received word,' sway sway, 'that there is a new chief guest due to hand out prizes at the National Oratory Competition.'

Hasan groaned. Javed laughed, 'Now I don't envy you any-more. We were all turning green, I swear, at the thought of you shaking hands with Razzledazzle.'

'To fit the new chief guest's schedule,' sway sway, 'the competition has been moved to May nineteenth.' Sway pause sway. 'The new chief guest is the President.'

May 19th. Eight days from now. Salman Mamoo's trial. The President shaking the hand of the competition winner. Was this a sign? A sign to remind him of everything the Oldest

Man had said? No. Forget spirits. Forget dolphins. Salman Mamoo will – say it! – die because the President doesn't like him. No need for rings of invisibility. A poem can bring me face to face with the President, and then. And then. I can do something.

'Not "Daffodils" again!' Javed moaned.

Nargis Lotia tip-toed circles on the stage, wandering lonely as a cloud, as she had done for the last four oratory competitions.

Hasan bent over and placed his head between his knees. The dragonflies sped up and began whirling frantically like dusk-fairies struggling to escape from between the enclosed palms of the Warlock. The thought of young Lochinvar coming out of the West held no interest for Hasan, which meant it would hold no interest for the audience either when he stood up to recite it. How would the President react to it? He'd probably applaud politely.

There was a poem Ami had book-marked in a magazine on her studio shelf. Each morning this last month Hasan had opened to the poem and found a new water-coloured finger-print on the page.

'Go on,' Javed nudged Hasan. 'Your turn.'

Hasan gripped the chair in front of him and rose to his feet. It was an English translation of a Turkish poem. Hasan formed an image of the fingerprinted page in his mind and scanned it as he walked towards the stage past row after row of grey and white uniforms. His hand reached into his trouser pocket and gripped a pine-cone. Lochinvar rode all alone and rode all unarmed clear out of Hasan's head. Hasan faced the crowd.

'"Some Advice to Those Who Will Serve Time in Prison" by Nazim Hikmet.' In the audience teachers exchanged concerned looks and students nudged each other, but it was too late to backtrack.

'If instead of being hanged by the neck
          you're thrown aside
          for not giving up hope
in the world, your country, and people,
          if you do ten or fifteen years
          apart from the time you have left,
you won't say,
                    "Better I had swung from the end of a rope
                    like a flag" –
you'll put your foot down and live.'

The words spilled out of him, gushed, tapered off, flowed, crashed down, the pauses and inflections instinctive things formed by Hasan and the crowd and transported through the air which now moved differently, not moved no!, more as though the air possessed strings perhaps, or ribbons of water which tied Hasan to the audience and carried, echoed, magnified each meaning created by the collision of words and moment.

'Part of you may live alone inside,
          like a stone at the bottom of a well.
But the other part
          must be so caught up
          in the flurry of the world
          that you shiver there inside
          when outside, at forty days' distance, a leaf
          moves.'

Forty days. Hasan visualized white sheets. Did the President have nephews? The page blanked in Hasan's mind. The ribbons of water disappeared. Hasan was alone, staring at the crowd – a boy who had forgotten his lines. The dusk-fairies were dead.

At the back of the auditorium Javed and Ayesha and Ali leaned forward as though they could restore the words to his mind if they could just narrow the gap between themselves and him. Hasan repeated the last lines in his mind to try and regain the flow. 'But the other part must be so caught up in the flurry of the world that you shiver there inside.' Hasan looked off to the side, where the broad-leafed almond tree spread its shadow over the tuck-shop. The ground around the tree was littered with smashed red fruit. Crows hopped around the fruit, pecking and cawing. Shiver, he told himself. There's reason enough, even without dolphins. Please God, I can't remember the words. Everyone's looking.

He would have liked, at least, to have walked off the stage with dignity, perhaps even a wry smile, but such considerations of panache were buried under his need to get off the stage, away from all those eyes as fast as possible. He ran down the steps and down the aisle, ignoring Nargis Lotia's outstretched hand and Javed's shrug of sympathy. Before he had even reached the last row of chairs Mrs Qureshi had ushered on the next orator with a speed she hadn't exhibited since the bomb scare two years earlier. Mrs D. Khan, spectacles glinting, was standing near the auditorium exit and made no attempt to stop Hasan as he ran out.

The gush from the water-cooler was brown, but at least it was cold enough to numb. Hasan bent his head under the tap and allowed the water to flow down skull, neck, spine. He stayed in that position long after the spigot spluttered and dried up, stayed there until Mrs Qureshi's voice from the auditorium announced that Nargis Lotia had won the school oratory competition with her excellent rendition of 'Daffodils'.

Hasan stumbled into the adjacent music room and curled up in a darkened corner against the piano legs. His sodden shirt clung to him and picked up dust and cobwebs from the piano's underside. Eight days eight days eight days eight days eight days. The pine-cone snapped in two between his trembling fists. Two boys, with the swagger of teenagers who have just started to shave, walked through the room.

'Well, do it soon then,' one of the boys said. 'Who knows how long school will be closed for riots and things when the trial starts. That's – what? – a week from now?'

'Eight days,' said the other. 'How long do you think they'll take to find him guilty? My father said trials can go on for months.'

'Nah! Not this one. Listen, I've heard when people are hanged their eyes pop out of their heads and their tongues get all black and swollen and twisted . . . oi!'

Hasan charged out of the building, pushing the boys to the side. He fell to his knees in the front yard, his hands braced against the white cement border of a flowerbed. His chest heaved and his face contorted. 'Don't die,' he sobbed, and it was only when he heard his voice that he knew he was crying at last. And then there was no stopping it; eyes and nose running faster than the back of his hand could wipe, 'don't die, please, don't die', hands raking through the flowerbed, plastering mud across face and hair, again and again, hands moving up from chin to scalp, stanching and reversing the trail of tears and snot, 'don't die don't die', a man alone in a grey-walled room hanging from a rope, a rope that did not swiftly snap a neck in two, but squeezed each breath by breath by gasping breath from the only lungs which knew just how to say 'Hasan' and make the name extraordinary.

Hasan's ribs hurt. The tears finally stopped but in their place came shuddering intakes of air. Hasan drew his legs up against his chest and encircled them with his arms so tightly there was no space for his heart to burst out. His trouser-band cut into his stomach, but breathing was already so difficult that it didn't matter. And then the gulping stopped too, and there started a different kind of crying. Grown-up tears which could trip out of wide-open eyes yet cause no tremor of voice. You could live with these tears all your life, Hasan thought, watching as the roots he had exposed in the flowerbed splintered and were whole, splintered and were whole, between the slide of one teardrop and the next. He plucked a serrated leaf off a shrub and wiped his nose with it. The action required all the energy and will-power he possessed.

Overhead, a whir of helicopter blades. The noise was a scattering of lead pencils across the sky. Hasan tried to imagine dragons and a blue tent but his head was throbbing. He really just wanted arms around him and voices, too, telling him 'Hey Hasan, Huss, *pehlvan*, son, knobble-knees, Hussy, my dear, *jaan*, it's okay' but it wasn't okay, it wasn't, and maybe it never would be.

Chapter Twenty-Four

Hasan watched honey from his teaspoon dribble back into the jar, creating serpent shapes which rapidly sank into the goo from which they had been created.

'If you've lost your appetite I'll lend you mine for a while,' Uncle Latif said, stretching across the verandah table to take the jar out of Hasan's hands and replace it with a piece of honeyed toast. 'Flexible repayment options. And no interest except self-interest. Which is to say, if you don't post that toast into your mouth, I will, and then I'll burst like a dream.'

Hasan pushed the plate away, and looked at his watch: 9.28 a.m. Salman Mamoo's trial would start at 10.00 a.m. That was the only information about the trial Aba's contacts had provided. Even the name of Salman Mamoo's lawyer, if he had one, remained encased in red-taped, top-level, security-sealed, unbribable secrecy.

Over the weekend, POTPAF (FKAACE) – Formally Known As ACE – had called for the City to show its moral fibre by going on strike once again to protest the trial; the government, in turn, had issued a statement declaring that there was no need to be cowed by terrorist demands; and private schools across the City had suddenly turned egalitarian and decided to create a Day of Reflection Concerning Privileges Of Private School Students, to be observed by staying at home and writing an essay about élitism, on Sunday, 19 May. According to the Bodyguard, many teachers and students at government-run schools were lending support to DORCPrOPriSS by staying at home too. As were Aba and Uncle Latif, though they didn't seem at all inclined to write essays or even help Hasan with his.

Only the Widow refused to be interrupted in her work; she had set off early this morning for the Shelter for Battered Women, just minutes after Khalida-the-Heartbreaker had driven up to the gate on – of all things – a motorcycle, with news that a teenaged widow had collapsed at the entrance to the shelter and asked for protection. Gul Mumani had gone with the Widow, and Zehra had wanted to accompany them too, but the Widow and Uncle Latif were adamant in their refusal to let her do so.

Hasan, hurt and somewhat offended that Zehra didn't seem to think it important to stay with him on the first day of the trial, had not been sympathetic. 'Battered Women sounds like something out of a cookbook,' he had said.

Zehra had kicked him. Very hard. 'The Widow opened the shelter, so shut up. And just shut up anyway.'

Hasan's shins still ached from the kick. He limped off the verandah, without a word to Uncle Latif, and adjusted the limp into a lurch when he saw Zehra walking towards him. She just rolled her eyes and headed for the breakfast tray.

Hasan climbed over the wall to his garden and heard, on the

street outside, a car brake to a stop. Somewhere, right now, someone in a uniform with gleaming buttons was opening the back door of a car. Salman Mamoo stepped out of the car in handcuffs, and smiled at the makeshift military courthouse before him the way a marathon runner might smile at the finish line without even knowing if he were the first or the last in the race to cross it. Salman Mamoo raised his hand and the wind carried the imprint of his palm to Hasan's cheek.

Hasan ran inside and picked up the telephone. His phonebook had a pencil marking the page with 'N' entries, but Hasan didn't even have to look at it. His finger jabbed at the phone digits in a 'P' formation and a man's voice answered on the other end.

'Hello . . . Hello? Anyone there?' A pause, and then: 'Whoever you are, you're very punctual. Every half hour on the dot. But take your talents elsewhere, or I'll get the operator to track you down.'

Hasan hung up, took a deep breath, and pressed redial. This time, when the voice answered he said, 'Hello, is Nargis there, please? This is Hasan.'

'Just a second,' the man said.

Hasan cradled the phone between ear and shoulder, and wiped his palms on his jeans. What was he going to say? Which of the two prepared speeches should he choose? The 'Come on, we both know I deserve it' speech or the 'Fate of the nation' speech.

'I'm sorry, Nargis can't come to the phone. She's getting ready for the Elocution Contest. You can watch it on television in . . . oh . . . just about an hour.'

Hasan nodded into the mouthpiece, wiped the receiver and hung up. This crying thing was getting ridiculous. He should never have allowed himself to start it in the schoolyard. He

195

should never have waited this long to speak to Nargis. He heard Ami calling to him, and ran into his room, where the magic place between the desk legs awaited him.

'Huss?'

Hasan was locked in battle with the Warlock when Ami's voice brought him back to his room. Ami opened the door to the room and walked in. Her footsteps walked right up to the desk. If she lifts up the sheet and destroys the magic, Hasan swore, I will hate her for ever.

Ami sat down, her back to Hasan's bookshelf. Only a few inches and a sheet separated her from Hasan, but she didn't look in his direction.

'I was just talking to Farah Apa. Your class teacher is a friend of hers,' she said. There were dots of blue paint on her cheek and Hasan knew she had absent-mindedly dipped the wrong end of her brush into her oils and, just seconds later, tapped the brush against her cheekbone as she considered her most recent brush strokes. Hasan slid his hand under the sheet and touched Ami's finger with his own.

'So,' Ami said. She bounced Hasan's palm off her own for a few seconds, then interlinked her fingers with his. 'What should we talk about?'

'I lied to you. Nargis wasn't better than me. I forgot my lines.'

'"She looked down to blush and she looked up to sigh with a smile on her lips and a tear in her eye,"' Ami quoted. 'There are worse things you could forget.' She smoothed down a scab on his knuckle which Hasan had been picking at.

'I wasn't doing "Lochinvar". I thought I had memorized the Hikmet poem but I blanked.'

'I see.' She turned her face towards him. 'And I believe Mrs Qureshi announced, prior to your recitation, that the

President would be the chief guest at the National Oratory Competition.'

Hasan pushed the sheet to a side and crawled out. 'Yes.'

Ami placed an arm around his shoulder and drew him close. 'Hasan, he has no conscience.'

'Everyone has a conscience.'

'No, his was surgically removed and replaced with paranoia. What's going on in your head these days?'

Hasan clenched his fist. How to tell her what he had done, what he hadn't done? 'I should have stuck with "Lochinvar". I would have won then, and I would have won the national competition too. And then I would have gone up to shake the President's hand and there would be no one, nothing, between us.'

Ami's arm stiffened. She caught his shoulders and leaned him backwards so he was forced to stare into her eyes. 'What would you have done then, Hasan?'

Hasan didn't know if it was Ami or himself that caused it to happen, but for the first time ever he could not read the expression in her voice. He wanted to cry again, but instead he stared defiantly back at her. 'It would have been, could have been my chance. I could have done something. Really done something. And it was so close, Ami. I'll never get a chance like that again. Not now. It's too late.'

Ami ducked her head and watched an ant swaying across the carpet beneath a crumb of bread. She was silent so long that Hasan's eyes started to droop. 'Hasan, did you see Azeem die?'

Her words hung in the air just like Azeem had. Hung suspended in a head-first, backwards dive long enough for Hasan to think, 'Oh God he's going to die God God he's going to die there's nothing I can do there'll never God oh God' but not long enough for him to look away.

197

Once upon a time there was a yellow kite, a laburnum tree, a moment of almost flight and a boy's head hitting the ground. Once upon a time a boy on a roof top saw a neck snap and the only word he could form in his mind was 'forever'.

'Yes,' Hasan said, constricting all his muscles. 'I saw it all.'

'Tell me.'

Those grown-up tears again. 'Maybe he was doing it, getting so involved in making the kite fly, because he knew I was watching.' He had never even thought the words before, but the moment they were out he knew them the way he might know his shadow if he bumped elbows with it in a dark place. Ami gripped his little finger, her head shaking no, my baby, sweetheart it's not your fault.

'It's not?' said Hasan. He pictured the boy so intent from the first on his battle with the wind that he didn't take his eyes off the kite long enough to blink. 'It's not.' Despite everything else that had happened, he felt as if a scorpion had crawled off his stomach. He rested his head on Ami's chest and let her heart pace his own out of its frantic thumping.

There followed the kind of silence that can only exist when another person helps to create it, and Hasan recalled the catch of breath with which he had yesterday woken from a dream of hands clasped in prayer which suddenly spread wide to release a cicada in the air. He knew it was a cicada, even though he had never seen a cicada, and he knew the cicada was miraculous though cicadas were not the stuff of miracles. At the moment of waking he felt that something close to perfection had just occurred and he cupped his hand over his heart so that the feeling would not leave him. Then, as now, the clock seemed to pause, just a fraction, between its ticks and its tocks.

The hallway door opened and two pairs of feet walked

through. Gul Mumani called out, 'Chalo, Sherry, Saira, next door. Latif's showing off his new TV. The President has landed, about to emerge from his hell-copter. Crowd of thousands to receive him, chanting his name. So touching, I swear.'

Aba came out of his bedroom. 'Crowd of thousands? How much do you think they're paid for their enthusiasm?'

'Dinner, probably,' said the Widow. 'Where are Saira and Hasan?'

'We'll join you there,' Ami yelled. The hall door swung closed behind Aba, and Ami began to hum a nursery rhyme. Hasan pressed a finger against her throat and felt her larynx vibrate as her voice rose and fell along a scale. 9.58 a.m.

The phone rang.

With the first sharp *trring*! Hasan knew it was Nargis Lotia calling, calling to say, 'I was about to leave the house, but I heard you rang. What's up?'

He knew it was her. Knew it as surely as he would later know that at the moment of that first *trring*! a girl was fighting her way through the helipad crowd to reach the President before he got into the black limousine surrounded by outriders on motorbikes.

Trring! Hasan sat up straight. It was not too late. It was not too late. He still remembered 'Lochinvar', and the Hikmet poem, too.

The girl tried to break past the police barrier, wilting flowers clutched in her hand. The President motioned the police to let her through.

Trring! Hasan stood up, thought of Salman Mamoo and dolphins.

The TV cameras zoomed in on the girl. The cameras caught a flash of green eyes.

Trring! Hasan walked towards the telephone. He thought of

Shehzad who might not have merely struck a match. Thought of Azeem. Thought, for some reason, of Aba and ice and string.

The President took the flowers with a smile. The girl's right hand was fisted. She opened the fist.

Trring! 'Well, are you answering it?' Ami said.

Something conical and segmented lay in the girl's palm. The dilation of the President's pupils gave the thing a name: grenade.

Trring! 'No,' Hasan said.

But really it was a pine-cone.

Hasan disconnected the phone. The girl turned and disappeared into the crowd.

Chapter Twenty-Five

'All at once I saw a crowd, a host of golden daffodils.' Hasan pressed a button on Uncle Latif's remote control and Nargis Lotia's face turned green. He pressed another button and her cheeks turned so red they started pulsing. Zehra grabbed the remote control and returned the image to normal.

'Ten thousand saw I at a glance . . .' Nargis Lotia stuck her head forward and opened her eyes wide wide.

Gul Mumani started out of her chair. 'We should be at home,' she said. 'Suppose someone calls. Someone . . . something about the trial.'

Aba held up his cordless phone. 'Thought of that. It's within range; it'll ring.'

Gul Mumani took the phone from him and held it to her ear. 'No tone!' she said. Aba pressed a button and Gul Mumani jerked her head away from the high-pitched hum of the phone. She switched the phone off, put it down, picked it up, switched it back on and dialled a number. The phone next to the Widow rang.

'Hello?' said the Widow into the receiver.

'Just checking,' Gul Mumani said. She seemed about to turn the phone off, but her finger froze an inch above the button. 'Will it ring if it's off?'

'For God's sake, Gul, relax,' Aba said, taking the phone from her, and punching the 'off' button with his finger. 'I said it'll ring, didn't I?'

'What's your problem, Shehryar? It's not as if you're never wrong,' Ami snapped.

'Now, now, folks and yolks,' Uncle Latif said. 'Shakespeare, isn't it? A child is a yolk?'

'Egg,' Aba said. 'Or young fry of treachery. Macbeth. Sorry, Gul.'

'It's the girl with the pine cone,' Zehra whispered to Hasan. 'She's made everyone jumpy. I wish you had seen her.'

Hasan looked across at Ami, who winked back.

'What's going on?' Zehra said, pointing to the television.

The camera was pulling back from Nargis Lotia's face, back and back so that the chicken pox scar above her eyebrow was no longer distinguishable; back to include all the contestants sitting on the stage to either side of Nargis; back to include the spectators turning their heads away from Nargis; and back further to include the two soldiers marching down the auditorium aisle towards the front row where the chief guest sat in a red velvet chair.

Nargis Lotia, once dubbed by a substitute teacher 'the sole mouse amongst a pack of rats', must have sensed her moment of fame being usurped by the uniformed men who didn't even attempt to muffle their footfall, because she screeched at the top of her lungs 'In vacant and in pensive mood!' The camera zoomed right back on to her face.

And so there was never any visual record of the President's

expression as he turned to hear what the soldier was whispering into his ear.

'The bliss of solitude,' Nargis finished, and glared at the cameraman so that even then he kept the lens trained on her while the audience applauded, then hesitated, then applauded some more. It was only after Nargis curtseyed and sat down that the camera pulled back again and Hasan saw the auditorium doors swinging, and a man in civilian dress sitting down in the red velvet chair.

Afterwards, everyone would have a story to tell about, or around, that day.

Ali Bhai would relate how he had seen several high-ranking military officers in whispered conversation with economic forecasters and financial strategists when he dropped in to pay a visit to General Jojo, just days before the Elocution Contest. '*Hanh*, okay, I didn't actually hear anything they said, if you must know the minute details, but the looks on their faces . . . those boys weren't just discussing the weather.'

Khan would say, yes, of course, the prospect of economic disaster was part of the reason for what happened. 'But not like your cousin Ali thinks, though maybe that was a part of it. The truth is, at the very moment the girl with the green eyes was opening her fist to the President, eight other people around the country were opening their fists to the President's eight advisors, and in each fist was a pine-cone. Each of these eight advisors called up the President while his limousine was taking him to the N. E. Uddin Auditorium for the Elocution Contest. By the time the sixth advisor called to say he had been handed a pine-cone while in the bathtub of his high-security mansion, the President knew he was being issued a final warning, and he didn't even wait for the eighth advisor to call from his secret getaway in the mountains before making a phone call to arrange for foreign asylum. No surprise really in what happened – any idiot could tell you that even if being barefoot is your biggest fear you don't exchange your car's engine for a pair of running shoes.'

Auntie Poops would dominate dinner party conversation for weeks with stories of how she was settling down in the business-class cabin of an aeroplane just prior to take-off, planning all the shopping she would do overseas, 'though of course it was hard to think of anything other than Saloo, with the trial starting and all. But then, be and lohold! in walked the Prezzie, flanked by two soldiers. On a commercial flight I swear. And not even First Class! So, of course, I scrambled off the plane and said to the airline people "minor heart-attack happening. Unload my luggage, pronto" which they weren't about to do until I showed them my profile which is a fax of my cousin's profile and, of course, she's married to that airline hotshot. Yes, sweetie, the Prezzie spoke before I left; he said, "Thank God I didn't have to sit through 'Daffodils'." Poor man, unhinged.'

Zehra, of course, would have her own version of events. 'See, stupid, the reason I wanted to go with the Widow to the shelter was that I was worried about her. I mean, I wouldn't leave you alone on the first day of Uncle Salman's trial just like that, okay?' Zehra rested her hand on Hasan's arm and he tried not to notice that she had waxed her arms and her skin no longer seemed that thing which he had so often seen scabbed and gashed and bloodied. The effort involved in not noticing Zehra's skin was so great that Hasan missed the first part of what she was saying about the early morning hours of 19 May, and only caught up with her story at the point when Gul Mumani was yelling at the Widow, 'Don't look at me so superior and manicured as if to say it's okay if my husband dies, at least I can dream of him. It's not okay, Widow-kiddo, not by a thousand leagues.' Ogle chose that moment to start barking hysterically and Zehra went outside to see what was bothering him. It was a chicken; a scrawny, beady-eyed fowl in no way deserving of a place in the tale. When Zehra shooed away the chicken and calmed down Ogle, she looked up to the Widow's balcony and – somehow Hasan never minded that Zehra thought what followed was the real story of the day – the Widow appeared on the balcony, feather pillow in one hand, knife glinting in the other. She slipped the pillow out of its case and held up the knife. In that moment the sun broke out of the clouds to glint off the knife and the Widow carefully placed the tip of the blade against the top corner of the pillow. Zehra looked up and screamed. The Widow slashed a diagonal, gripped the fabric on either side of the tear and ripped the pillow apart.

The feathers flew out, caught a violent gust of breeze and swirled over Zehra, over Hasan's house, over Azeem's rooftop, eddying and twirling dervish dances in the City of no snow, encore after encore until the breeze dropped. The feathers landed on soldiers, economists, ACEmen, the Bodyguard, artists, lawyers, suits, *shalwars*, a helicopter and a green-eyed girl, and blanketed the City with dreams of love.

After all, Zehra said, why not?

Why not? Hasan repeated, and never added, It's a good sub-plot.

The main plot? Some days he could not bring himself to talk of it, just as Shah Jahan could not bring himself to look directly at the Taj. On those days, Hasan understood what Ami had meant when she said that there are memories that cannot be spoken of, because to speak of them imperfectly is to rob them of something vital, though to leave them intact, inside, is to leave no space for anything else in your life. On the days when he believed this, Hasan would go to a dictionary and look for words that could first lacerate his tongue, then bind the gashes with blood. Words which were music and picture and meaning at once. Like 'lacerate', like 'cinnamon', like 'touch'.

Other days, Hasan would say just this: on 19 May, a little before sunset, I was crossing from my parents' room to my bedroom when the hall door opened and a voice said the most extraordinary thing:

'Hasan.'

Epilogue

The City air whispered of mangoes.

The first fruits of the season had ripened to pungent sweet-sourness, and the scent was so dizzying Hasan would have fallen off the branches of Uncle Latif's mango tree if Salman Mamoo had not been sitting behind him on the tree limb, holding him around the waist with one arm while the other arm pulled fruit-laden branches towards Hasan's nose and made him dizzier still.

'Stop,' Hasan laughed. 'Stop or I'll . . .' He reached back to try and pinch Salman Mamoo's nose shut, and his fingers brushed against a razor cut, one of several that Salman Mamoo had acquired over the past two days while trying to adjust to blades that weren't dulled by rust. This morning Hasan had seen a dot of blood on Salman Mamoo's sink, glistening. Hasan took the blood on his lips, and passed it down to his tongue and his tooth. Only then could he stop pretending that a part of him was prepared for armed guards to drag Salman Mamoo back to prison, and he knelt on the bathroom floor and touched his forehead to the tiles.

But there was still one thing he needed to know. 'Mamoojaan?' he said.

Salman Mamoo plucked a paisley shaped mango off its branch and cut away flesh from seed with his penknife, his forearms still gripping Hasan's waist. 'What is it?' he said, giving Hasan one 'cheek' of the mango.

'The green-eyed girl,' Hasan said. He took the penknife from Salman Mamoo, sliced the cheek in two, lengthwise, placed his thumbnail between the skin and the pulp of one slice and eased off the skin, making sure no pulp stayed attached to the skin during the separation. 'She could have got in trouble, couldn't she? I mean, just for having a pine-cone, let alone for being suspected of having a grenade. All those armed soldiers around and everything.'

'Yes,' Salman Mamoo said.

'So why do you think she did it?' Hasan slid his thumb across the smoothness of the pulp where the penknife had sliced, while his fingers caressed the slightly coarser underside of the mango-wedge where fibres had connected flesh to skin. He knew if he turned his head he would see Salman Mamoo's lips composing a dolphin metaphor.

Salman Mamoo said, 'I don't think she knew what she was doing.'

Mango juice was trickling down Hasan's palm, but he ignored it and turned his head to look out on the street where a beige car with a cracked windshield was parked. Salman Mamoo leaned back against the tree-trunk and clenched his fist.

Hasan bit into his mango and leapt down from the tree. 'Okay,' he said, staring up at Salman Mamoo, arms akimbo.

'Enough of this. Don't think I haven't noticed. Worrying about Shehzad and his faction, worrying about the military, worrying about pend . . . pending . . .'

'Pendular time,' Salman Mamoo said, swinging himself off the tree. 'The inability of democracies to succeed in this country. The cycle of failure.'

'Yeah, that,' Hasan said. 'You can do a wheelie on a cycle. I'll teach you.' And silently he added, Just let today be perfect.

Salman Mamoo took Hasan's hand, the mango stains on both their palms meshing like jigsaw pieces. Together they walked towards the front garden, where Ami, Aba, Gul Mumani, the Widow and Zehra were sitting in a circle watching the sunset.

'Here he is,' Aba said. 'The Salamander. We've decided your party needs a new name. Elections are eighty-eight days away and I, for one, refuse to vote for a party called POTPAF. And let's face it, much as I like Star Trek, the Anti-Corruption Enterprise didn't thrill me either.'

Salman Mamoo laughed. 'The party votes on a new name tomorrow. We've had some suggestions already. The best one is Party of Integrity and National Empowerment.'

'Ugh!' said Ami. 'How . . . oh, I see – PINE.'

'Yes,' said Salman Mamoo. 'We've got the acronym. We just need the words to fit the initials. Suggestions?'

'Please, I Need Electing,' said Ami.

'Prayer Is Not Enough,' Gul Mumani added.

'President Is Now Ejected,' Hasan volunteered.

The corners of Salman Mamoo's mouth twitched. He turned away to hide his expression and a pine-cone from a passing car hurtled over the wall and smacked him in the face. 'I'll say this much for the last few months,' he said, sticking the pine-cone behind his ear. 'They've made me understand how this City can get under your skin, and never be sweated out. I mean, it's still aesthetically traumatic, but it's got spirit.'

'About time,' Ami snorted. 'You've finally recovered from Wordsworth. I may vote for you after all.'

With great dignity, Salman Mamoo stuck out his tongue at Ami. 'I don't need your vote, thank you. Polls show that ACEPOTPAFPINE is headed to a landslide victory. Of course, once we win . . .' He sighed and passed a hand over his eyes.

The Widow cleared her throat.

'Yes, Wid?' Salman Mamoo said.

'Hina,' said the Widow.

'Henna? Yes,' Salman Mamoo said, looking at her hair. 'Yes, it's not as bright as usual, but . . .'

'Oh, shut up Salman!' Gul Mumani laughed. 'That's her name.'

'But we can still call her "Wid" if we want to,' Zehra told Hasan.

'Hina.' Salman Mamoo tried out the name a few times in different tones of voice, and nodded, satisfied. 'It suits you. So has my wife convinced you to help out with her schools?'

'*Na, baba*, she has other plans,' Gul Mumani grinned. 'They might interest you.'

'Oh, what?'

'Well, I'm considering three options really,' the Widow said. 'One, to join your party and become Minister of Law when you come into power. Two, to form my own party and stand against you. Three, to stay out of organized politics and create a non-government organization that will be involved in various developmental projects and will rant and rave against the powers-that-be whenever that seems necessary. Close your mouth, Salman, you don't look dignified.' The Widow, it appeared, had lied about the feather pillow and death. Hasan thought about it and decided he didn't mind that it had been a lie. He didn't mind at all.

'You're serious!' Salman Mamoo said.

'Of course I'm serious, Salman,' the Widow said, leaning sideways and smiling at Salman Mamoo, elbow crooked on the backrest of her chair. 'I realize if I choose Option Two I'll have limited short-term success, but you know what the wonderful thing about democracy is?'

'What?'

'Re-elections in five years. Wait. I've got it. I'll start with Option Three and build up a level of visibility that will help me with Option Two when the next election rolls around. Though if you really beg, I might be persuaded to give more thought to Option One.'

Salman Mamoo ruffled his eyebrows and stared at the Widow. 'I'll bear that in mind.' He grinned, his old boyish grin. 'You may be just the thing to throw a pendulum out of whack.'

The evening had become night with its usual mixture of subtlety and suddenness, and Uncle Latif danced into the garden, holding up to Salman Mamoo a contract for advertising pine-scented air-freshener.

'*Suno*, Salman, I've thrown in a clause, my own brilliant inspiration unaided by all except the Divine, stating – see page two, para three – that you may use eight seconds of advertising time to ask for votes. Or, conversely, spout the following lines mixing politics and salesmanship which, let's face it, is always the case: "Don't desist from voting for me because of fear of election booths reeking of body odour. Instead, buy Latifbhai's pine-scented air-freshener and spray it liberally through the booth for your benefit, and the benefit of fellow voters." This is serious!'

211

Hasan cut and peeled the rest of the mango that Salman Mamoo had plucked, and handed Zehra a slice, even though she had been talking to Najam on the phone earlier today. He wondered if she knew how much that annoyed him. Probably. Ogle sniffed a piece of mango skin, and began to lick it. Sighs from outside signalled that the Bodyguard, Imran and Aqib were finishing up their own meal of mangoes, all rivalries and bickering put aside for the moment. Hasan hauled himself up and climbed over the wall to examine the looks of contentment on the faces outside.

'If the world must end, let it be now,' Khan said.

Someone Hasan had never seen before was seated with the Bodyguard. Khan's sister, Hasan realized, looking at her features and her reddish-brown hair. Even though her hand was somewhat obscured Hasan was sure she had a rectangle of paper, covered in newsprint, wrapped around her finger like a wedding ring.

Not now, Hasan told himself. Not now.

He slipped back to his side of the wall, and climbed the spiral staircase to the roof. For a long time he just sat there, watching the two circles of people, catching traces of conversation, waving down at Salman Mamoo when Zehra pointed out where Hasan had disappeared to.

Eventually he stood up, gazed for a moment at Azeem's roof, and then descended the stairs. Was any of it true? he wondered on his way down. Any of what the Oldest Man had told him about spirits and death?

'If so, what does my spirit want?'

He stood in his garden, looked up at the stars, impossibly distant, and felt again that oldest desire: to touch the sky.

'But I can't,' he said. 'Unless I learn to shoot down the sky.' And then: 'Or . . .'

Hasan scrunched his eyes tight tight tighter, bent his knees in a diver's crouch, his arms extending backwards. 'Now!' he breathed. He jumped straight up into the night, his hands a pendulum cutting down in the air and then back up again, up in front of his body. The pendulum reached its maximum height, began its downward journey, but no! someone, some-how, caught his hands: Khan's-brother-in-law-Azeem-the-green-eyed-girl reached down from the stars and grabbed his hands, pulled them further up, beyond the limits of the pendulum's parabola. The moon glowed behind his eyelids, the wind rushed around him, something – a star! – cut against his palm. He whirled, twirled, felt beneath his fingers: charcoal doll's hair stalactite.

And Hasan was night.

Acknowledgements

Thanks to the following people who, either directly or in some tangential way, made this book possible: Agha Sahid Ali; Alexandra Pringle; John Edgar Wideman; Noy Holland; Shona Ramaya; the Fiction Babes – Tamara Grogan, Lesley Hyatt, Justine Dymond, Therese Chehade and, in particular, Elizabeth Porto; Herman Fong; Karin Gosselink; Brion Dulac; Tushna Kandawalla; and, foremost, Asad Haider.

ALSO AVAILABLE BY KAMILA SHAMSIE

HOME FIRE

Winner of the Women's Prize 2018

'Breathtaking' **ALI SMITH** 'Powerful' **GUARDIAN** 'Fearless' **THE TIMES**

How can love survive betrayal? For as long as they can remember, siblings Isma, Aneeka and Parvaiz have had nothing but each other. But darker, stronger forces will divide Parvaiz from his sisters and drive him to the other side of the world, as he sets out to fulfil the dark legacy of the jihadist father he never knew.

'A timely rejoinder to all the cant and prejudice. An intelligent, thought-provoking and beautifully written novel about family, identity and divided loyalties'
MAIL ON SUNDAY

'Brave and brilliant ... shocking and strangely beautiful'
SUNDAY TIMES

'Fearless but hugely troubling ... One pays it the highest compliment one can pay fiction: it makes you think. Uncomfortably'
THE TIMES

ORDER YOUR COPY:

BY PHONE: +44 (0) 1256 302 699; BY EMAIL: DIRECT@MACMILLAN.CO.UK
DELIVERY IS USUALLY 3–5 WORKING DAYS. FREE POSTAGE AND PACKAGING FOR ORDERS OVER £20.
ONLINE: WWW.BLOOMSBURY.COM/BOOKSHOP
PRICES AND AVAILABILITY SUBJECT TO CHANGE WITHOUT NOTICE.

WWW.BLOOMSBURY.COM/AUTHOR/KAMILA-SHAMSIE

BLOOMSBURY

A GOD IN EVERY STONE

Shortlisted for the Baileys Women's Prize for Fiction

Summer, 1914. Young Englishwoman Vivian Rose Spencer is in an ancient land, about to discover the Temple of Zeus, the call of adventure, and love. Thousands of miles away a twenty-year-old Pathan, Qayyum Gul, is learning about brotherhood and loyalty in the British Indian army. Summer, 1915. Viv has been separated from the man she loves; Qayyum has lost an eye at Ypres. They meet on a train to Peshawar, unaware that a connection is about to be forged between their lives – one that will reveal itself fifteen years later when anti-colonial resistance, an ancient artefact and a mysterious woman will bring them together again.

'First-rate – intelligent, vivid and completely absorbing'
DAILY MAIL

'I can't recommend *A God in Every Stone* by Kamila Shamsie too strongly ... Exciting and, in the end, profoundly moving, this will solace you during the grimmest holiday'
ANTONIA FRASER, *GUARDIAN* SUMMER READING

'A magnificent novel: beautiful, terrible, true ... It reads already like a classic'
ALI SMITH

ORDER YOUR COPY:

BY PHONE: +44 (0) 1256 302 699; **BY EMAIL:** DIRECT@MACMILLAN.CO.UK
DELIVERY IS USUALLY 3–5 WORKING DAYS. FREE POSTAGE AND PACKAGING FOR ORDERS OVER £20.
ONLINE: WWW.BLOOMSBURY.COM/BOOKSHOP
PRICES AND AVAILABILITY SUBJECT TO CHANGE WITHOUT NOTICE.

WWW.BLOOMSBURY.COM/AUTHOR/KAMILA-SHAMSIE

B L O O M S B U R Y